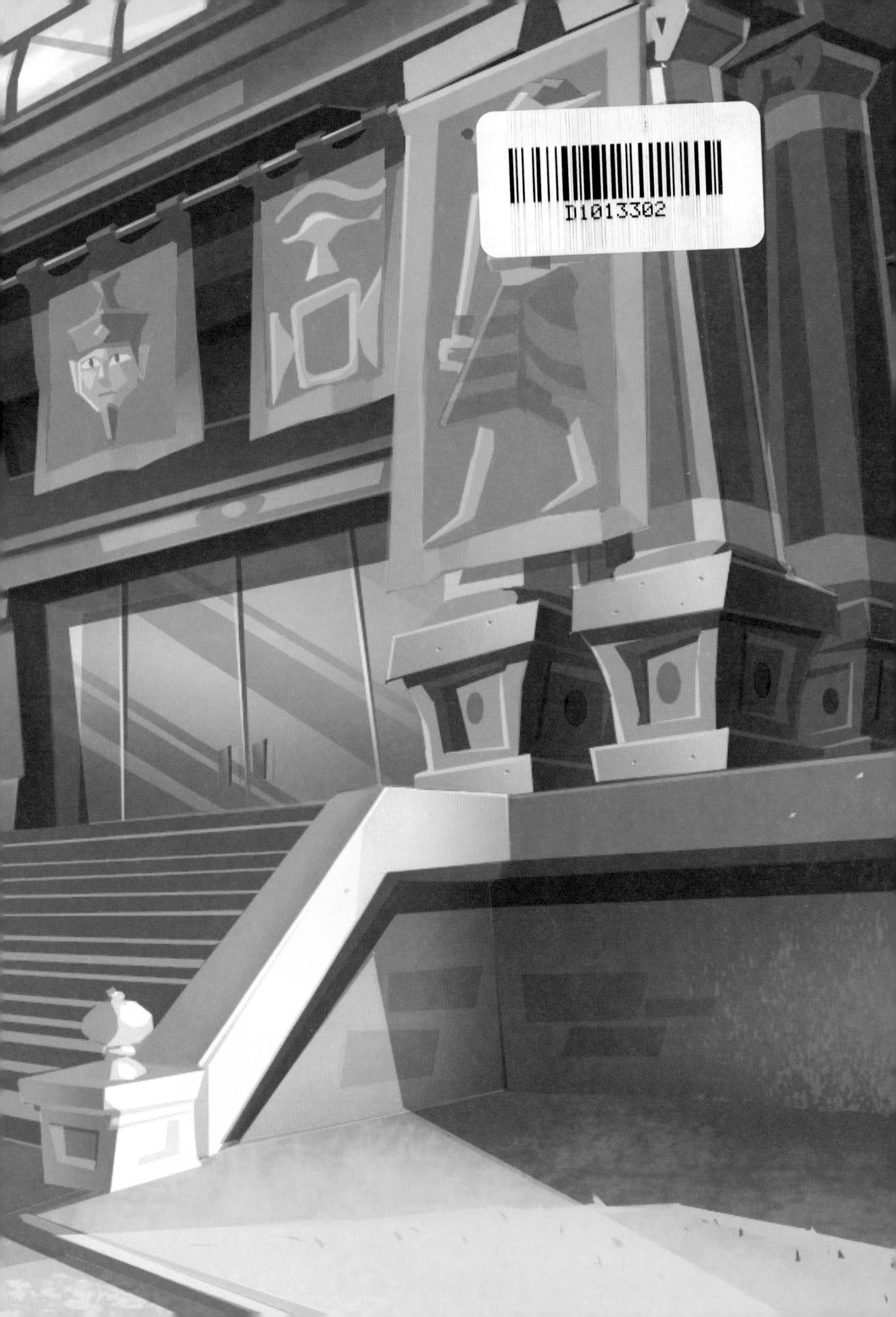

Geronimo Stilton

GRAPHIC NOVELS AVAILABLE FROM PAPERCUT

#1
"The Discovery
of America"

#2
"The Secret
of the Sphinx"

#3
"The Coliseum
Con"

#4
"Following the
Trail of Marco Polo"

#5
"The Great
Ice Age"

#6
"Who Stole
The Mona Lisa?"

#7
"Dinosaurs
in Action"

#8
"Play It Again,
Mozart!"

#9
"The Weird
Book Machine"

#10
"Geronimo Stilton
Saves the Olympics"

#11
"We'll Always
Have Paris"

#12
"The First Samurai"

#13
"The Fastest Train
in the West"

#14
"The First Mouse
on the Moon"

#15
"All for Stilton,
Stilton for All!"

#16
"Lights, Camera,
Stilton!"

#17
"The Mystery of the
Pirate Ship"

#18
"First to the Last Place
on Earth"

#19
"Lost in Translation"

GERONIMO
STILTON REPORTER #1
"Operation ShuFongFong"

GERONIMO
STILTON REPORTER #2
"It's My Scoop"

GERONIMO
STILTON REPORTER #3
"Stop Acting Around"

GERONIMO
STILTON REPORTER #4
"The Mummy with No Name"

COMING SOON

GERONIMO
STILTON REPORTER #5
"Barry the Moustache"

...ALSO AVAILABLE WHEREVER E-BOOKS ARE SOLD!

See more at papercutz.com

GERONIMO STILTON
3 in 1 #1

GERONIMO STILTON
3 in 1 #2

GERONIMO STILTON
3 in 1 #3

Geronimo Stilton™ Reporter

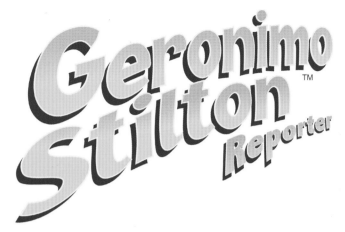

#4 THE MUMMY WITH NO NAME

By Geronimo Stilton

PAPERCUTZ™
NEW YORK

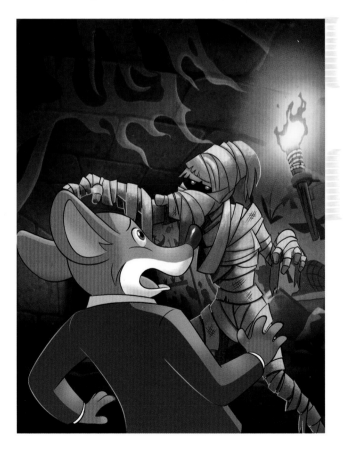

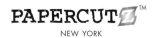

THE MUMMY WITH NO NAME
Geronimo Stilton names, characters and related indicia are copyright, trademark and exclusive license of Atlantyca S.p.A.
All right reserved.
The moral right of the author has been asserted.

Text by Geronimo Stilton
Cover by ALESSANDRO MUSCILLO (artist) and CHRISTIAN ALIPRANDI (colorist)
Editorial supervision by ALESSANDRA BERELLO (Atlantyca S.p.A.)
Editing by LISA CAPIOTTO (Atlantyca S.p.A.)
Script by DARIO SICCHIO based on the episode by KURT WELDON
Art by ALESSANDRO MUSCILLO
Color by CHRISTIAN ALIPRANDI
Original Lettering by MARIA LETIZIA MIRABELLA

TM & © Atlantyca S.p.A. Animated Series © 2010 Atlantyca S.p.A.– All Rights Reserved
© 2020 for this Work in English language by Papercutz, 160 Broadway, Suite 700, East Wing, New York, NY 10038
www.papercutz.com

Based on an original idea by ELISABETTA DAMI.
Based on episode 4 of the Geronimo Stilton animated series "La Mummia Senza Nome."

www.geronimostilton.com

Stilton is the name of a famous English cheese. It is a registered trademark of the Stilton Cheese Makers' Association.
For more information go to www.stiltoncheese.com

JAYJAY JACKSON — Production
WILSON RAMOS JR. — Lettering
IZZY BOYCE-BLANCHARD — Editorial Intern
JEFF WHITMAN — Managing Editor
JIM SALICRUP
Editor-in-Chief

ISBN: 978-1-5458-0402-5

Printed in China
January 2020

Papercutz books may be purchased for business or promotional use.
For information on bulk purchases please contact
Macmillan Corporate and Premium Sales
Department at (800) 221-7945x5442.

Distributed by Macmillan
First Printing

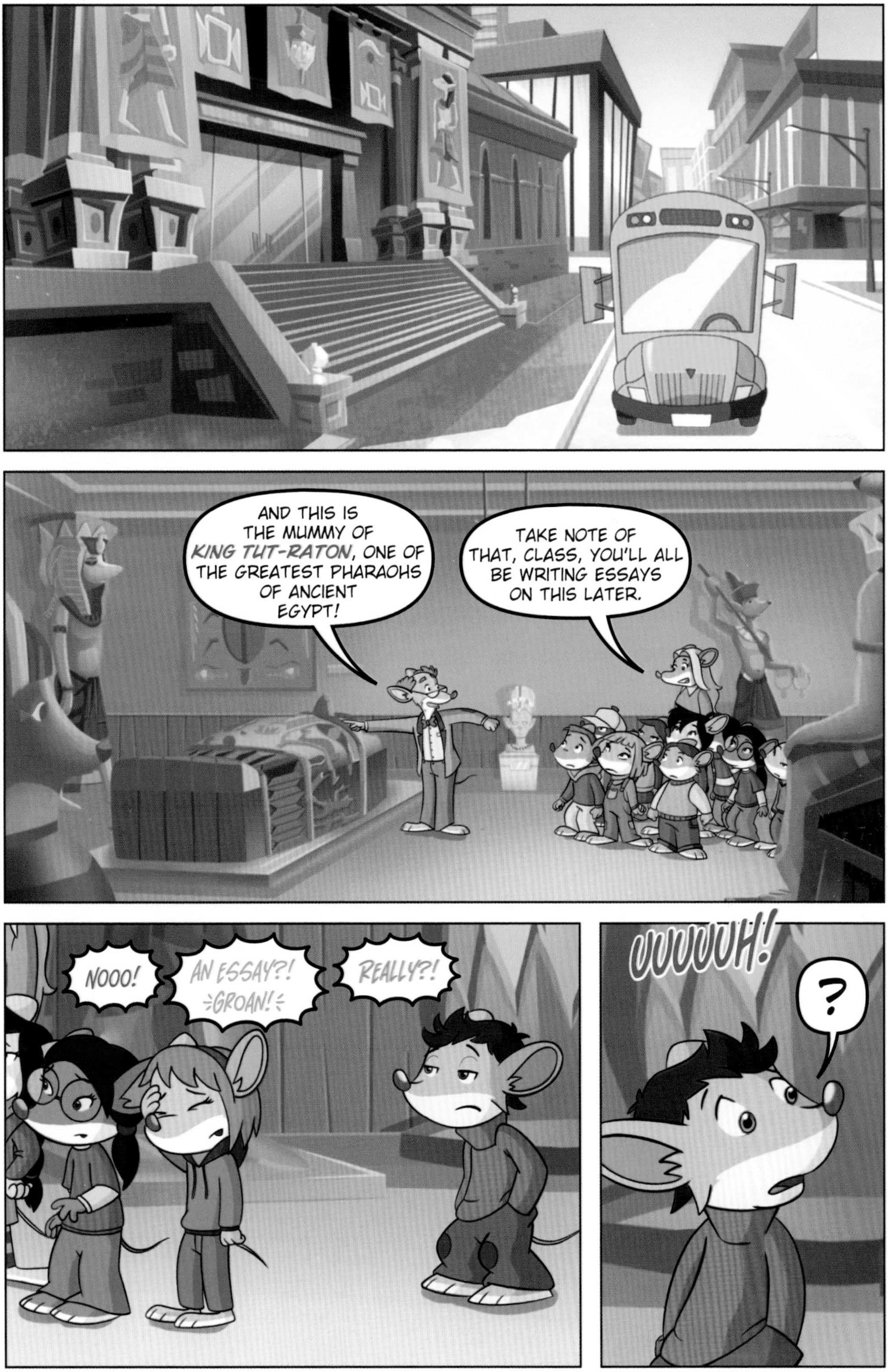
AND THIS IS THE MUMMY OF KING TUT-RATON, ONE OF THE GREATEST PHARAOHS OF ANCIENT EGYPT!
TAKE NOTE OF THAT, CLASS, YOU'LL ALL BE WRITING ESSAYS ON THIS LATER.
NOOO!
AN ESSAY?! GROAN!
REALLY?!
UUUUUH!
?

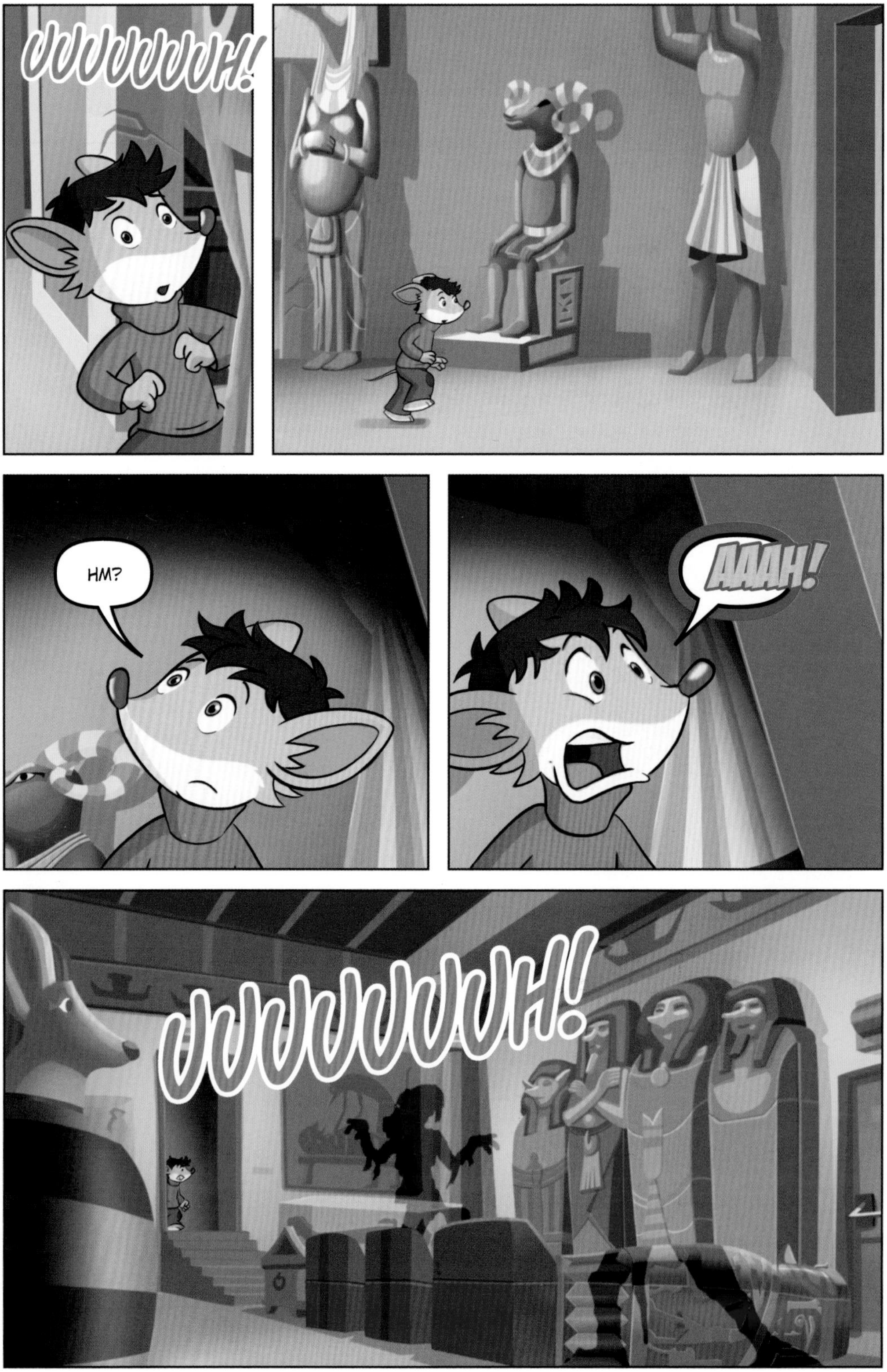
UUUUUUUH!
HM?
AAAH!
UUUUUUUUH!

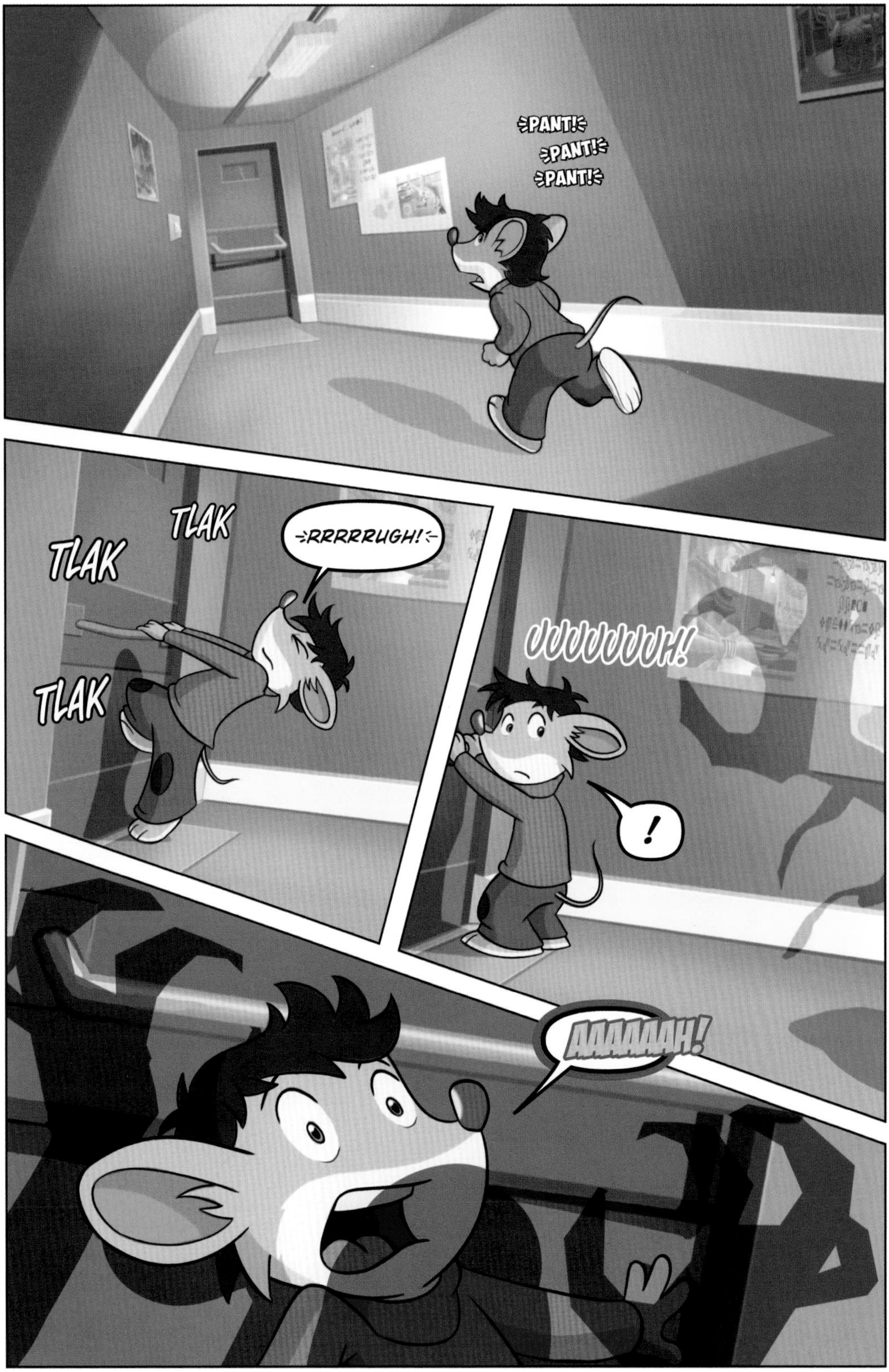
PANT!
PANT!
PANT!
TLAK
TLAK
RRRRRUGH!
TLAK
UUUUUUUH!
!
AAAAAAH!

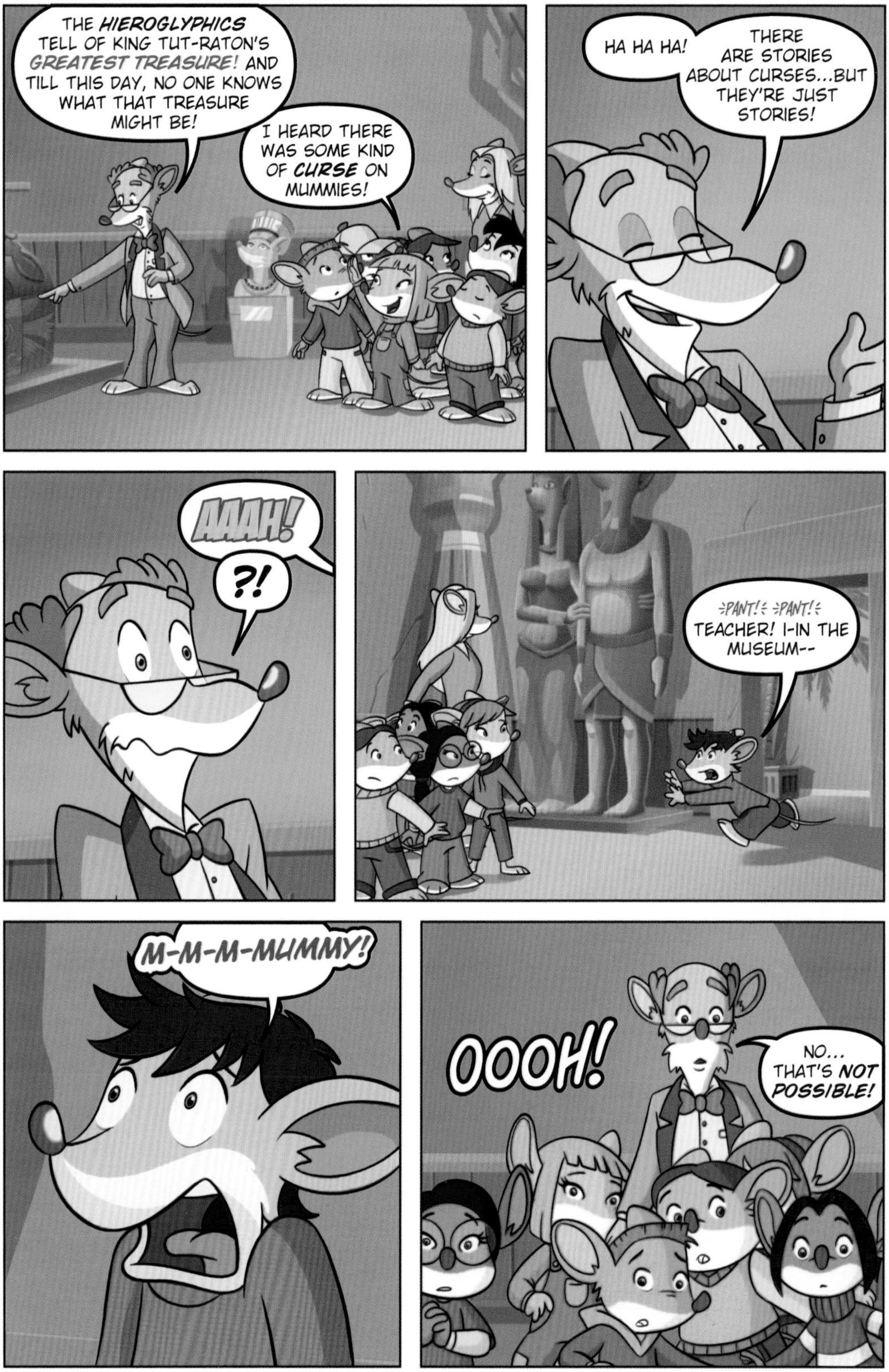
THE **HIEROGLYPHICS** TELL OF KING TUT-RATON'S **GREATEST TREASURE!** AND TILL THIS DAY, NO ONE KNOWS WHAT THAT TREASURE MIGHT BE!
I HEARD THERE WAS SOME KIND OF **CURSE** ON MUMMIES!
HA HA HA!
THERE ARE STORIES ABOUT CURSES...BUT THEY'RE JUST STORIES!
AAAH!
?!
PANT! PANT!
TEACHER! I-IN THE MUSEUM--
M-M-M-MUMMY!
OOOH!
NO... THAT'S **NOT POSSIBLE!**

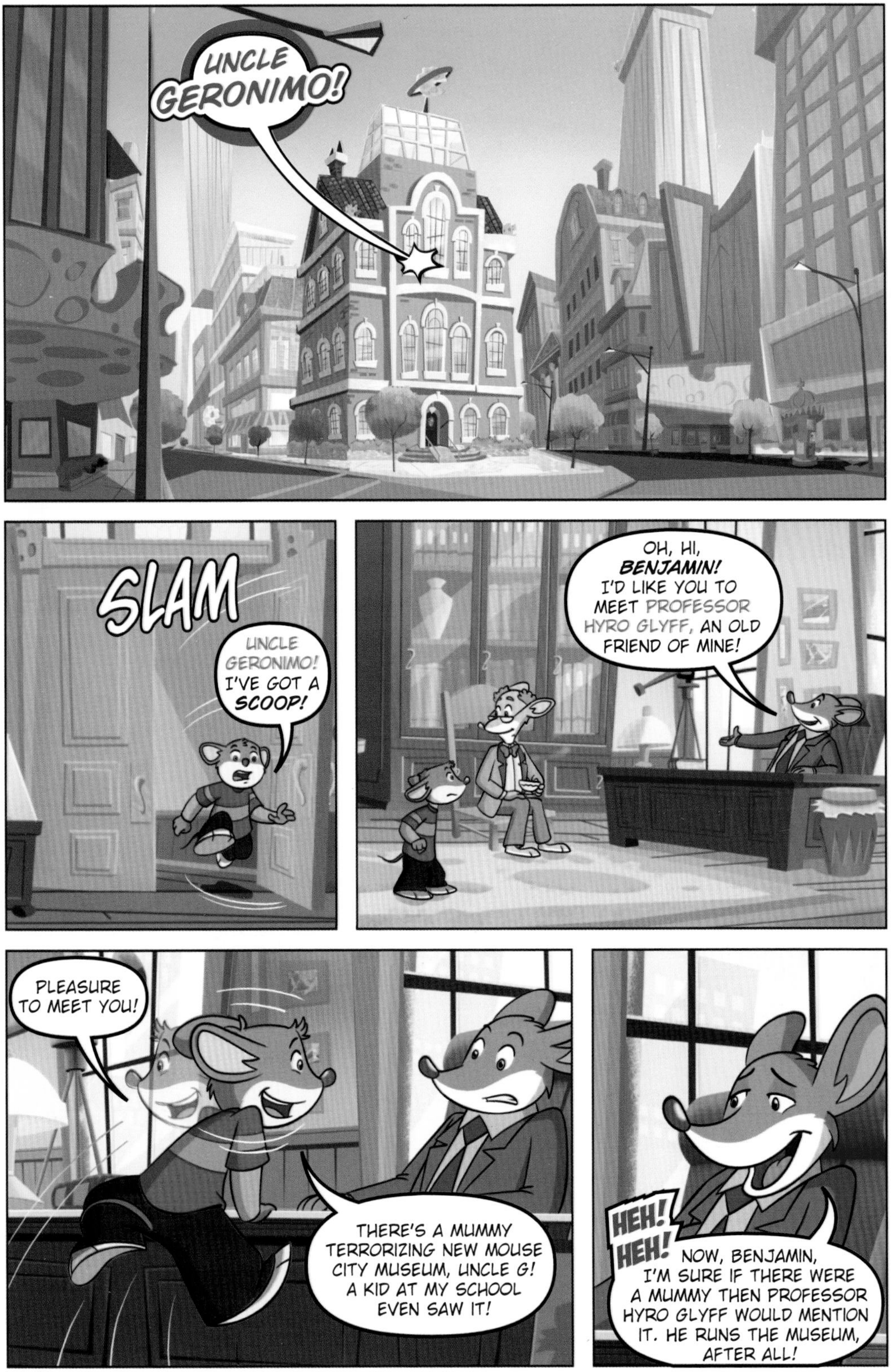
UNCLE GERONIMO!
SLAM
UNCLE GERONIMO! I'VE GOT A SCOOP!
OH, HI, BENJAMIN! I'D LIKE YOU TO MEET PROFESSOR HYRO GLYFF, AN OLD FRIEND OF MINE!
PLEASURE TO MEET YOU!
THERE'S A MUMMY TERRORIZING NEW MOUSE CITY MUSEUM, UNCLE G! A KID AT MY SCHOOL EVEN SAW IT!
HEH! HEH!
NOW, BENJAMIN, I'M SURE IF THERE WERE A MUMMY THEN PROFESSOR HYRO GLYFF WOULD MENTION IT. HE RUNS THE MUSEUM, AFTER ALL!

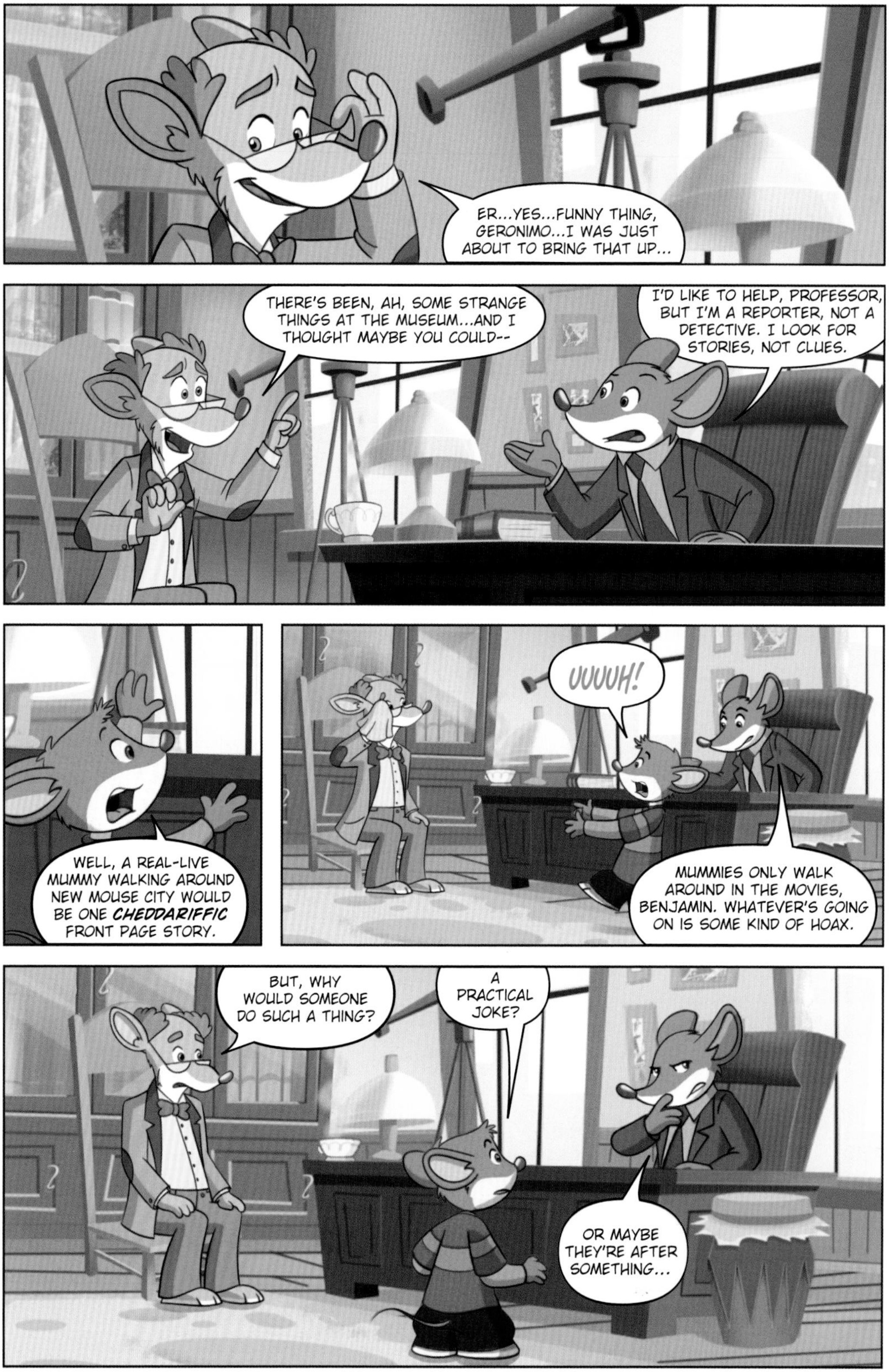
ER...YES...FUNNY THING, GERONIMO...I WAS JUST ABOUT TO BRING THAT UP...
THERE'S BEEN, AH, SOME STRANGE THINGS AT THE MUSEUM...AND I THOUGHT MAYBE YOU COULD--
I'D LIKE TO HELP, PROFESSOR, BUT I'M A REPORTER, NOT A DETECTIVE. I LOOK FOR STORIES, NOT CLUES.
WELL, A REAL-LIVE MUMMY WALKING AROUND NEW MOUSE CITY WOULD BE ONE ***CHEDDARIFFIC*** FRONT PAGE STORY.
UUUUH!
MUMMIES ONLY WALK AROUND IN THE MOVIES, BENJAMIN. WHATEVER'S GOING ON IS SOME KIND OF HOAX.
BUT, WHY WOULD SOMEONE DO SUCH A THING?
A PRACTICAL JOKE?
OR MAYBE THEY'RE AFTER SOMETHING...

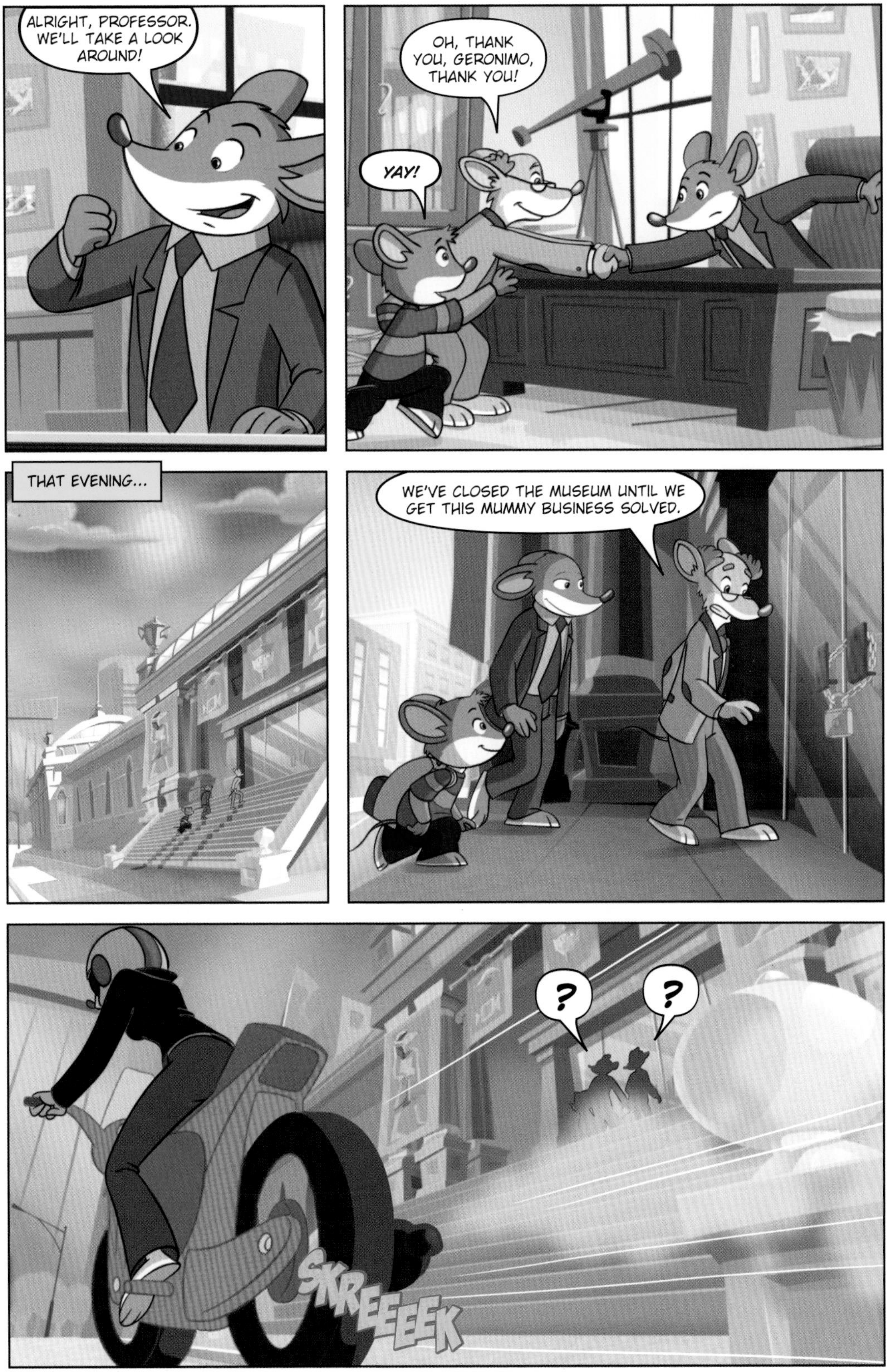
ALRIGHT, PROFESSOR. WE'LL TAKE A LOOK AROUND!
OH, THANK YOU, GERONIMO, THANK YOU!
YAY!
THAT EVENING...
WE'VE CLOSED THE MUSEUM UNTIL WE GET THIS MUMMY BUSINESS SOLVED.
?
?
SKREEEEK

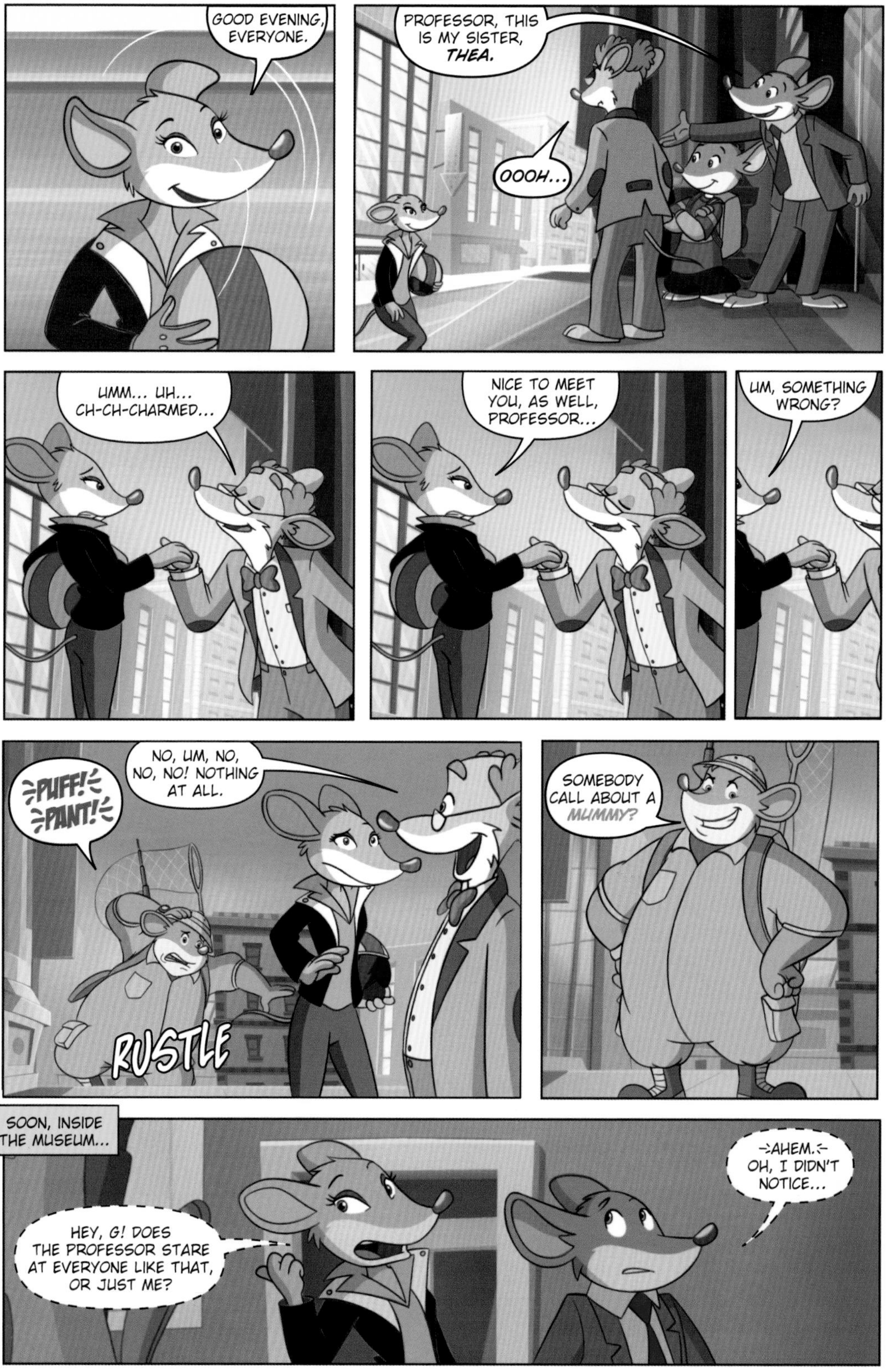
GOOD EVENING, EVERYONE.
PROFESSOR, THIS IS MY SISTER, THEA.
OOOH...
UMM... UH... CH-CH-CHARMED...
NICE TO MEET YOU, AS WELL, PROFESSOR...
UM, SOMETHING WRONG?
PUFF! PANT!
NO, UM, NO, NO, NO! NOTHING AT ALL.
RUSTLE
SOMEBODY CALL ABOUT A MUMMY?
SOON, INSIDE THE MUSEUM...
HEY, G! DOES THE PROFESSOR STARE AT EVERYONE LIKE THAT, OR JUST ME?
AHEM. OH, I DIDN'T NOTICE...

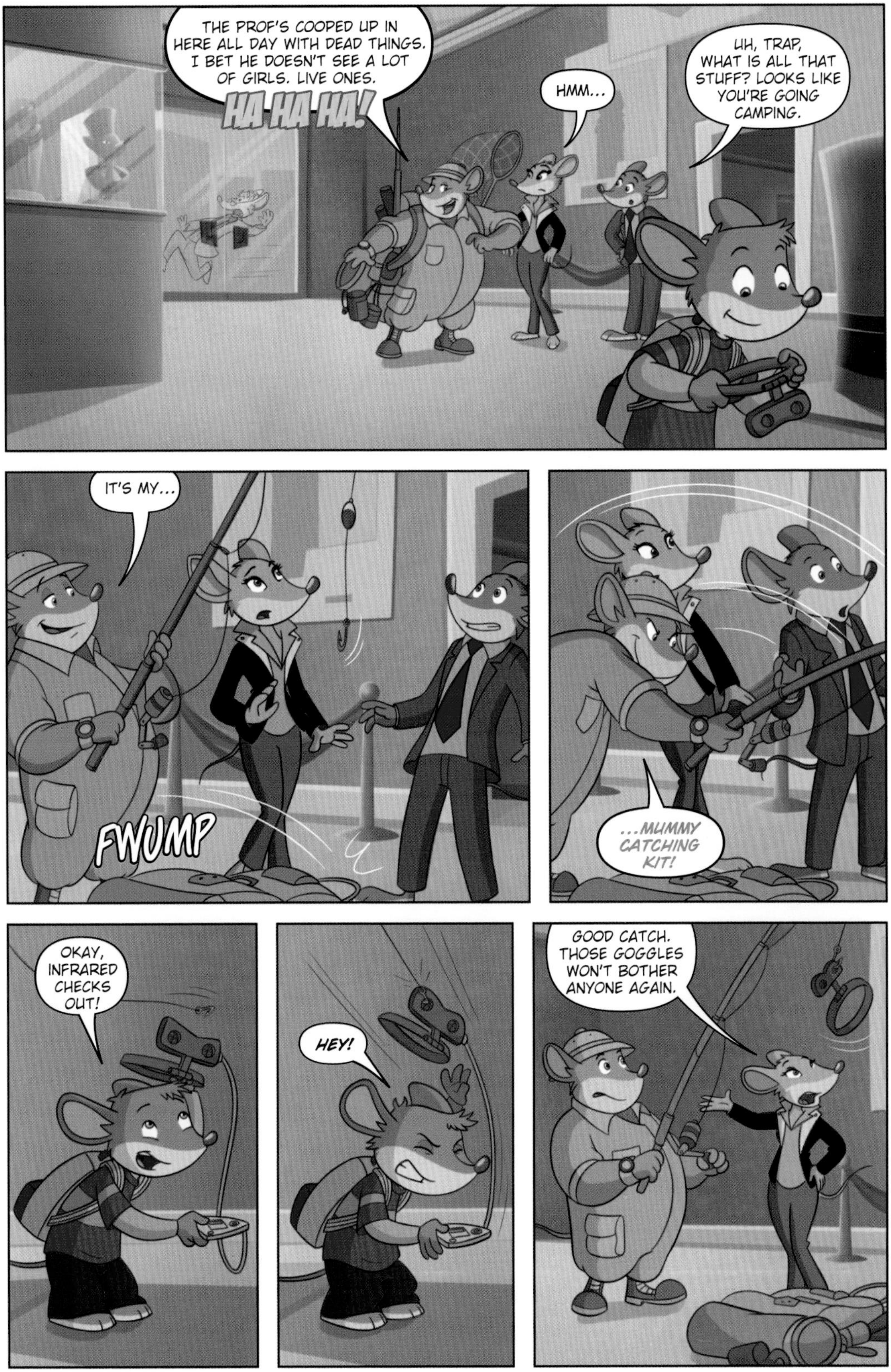
THE PROF'S COOPED UP IN HERE ALL DAY WITH DEAD THINGS. I BET HE DOESN'T SEE A LOT OF GIRLS. LIVE ONES.
HA HA HA!
HMM...
UH, TRAP, WHAT IS ALL THAT STUFF? LOOKS LIKE YOU'RE GOING CAMPING.
IT'S MY...
FWUMP
...MUMMY CATCHING KIT!
OKAY, INFRARED CHECKS OUT!
HEY!
GOOD CATCH. THOSE GOGGLES WON'T BOTHER ANYONE AGAIN.

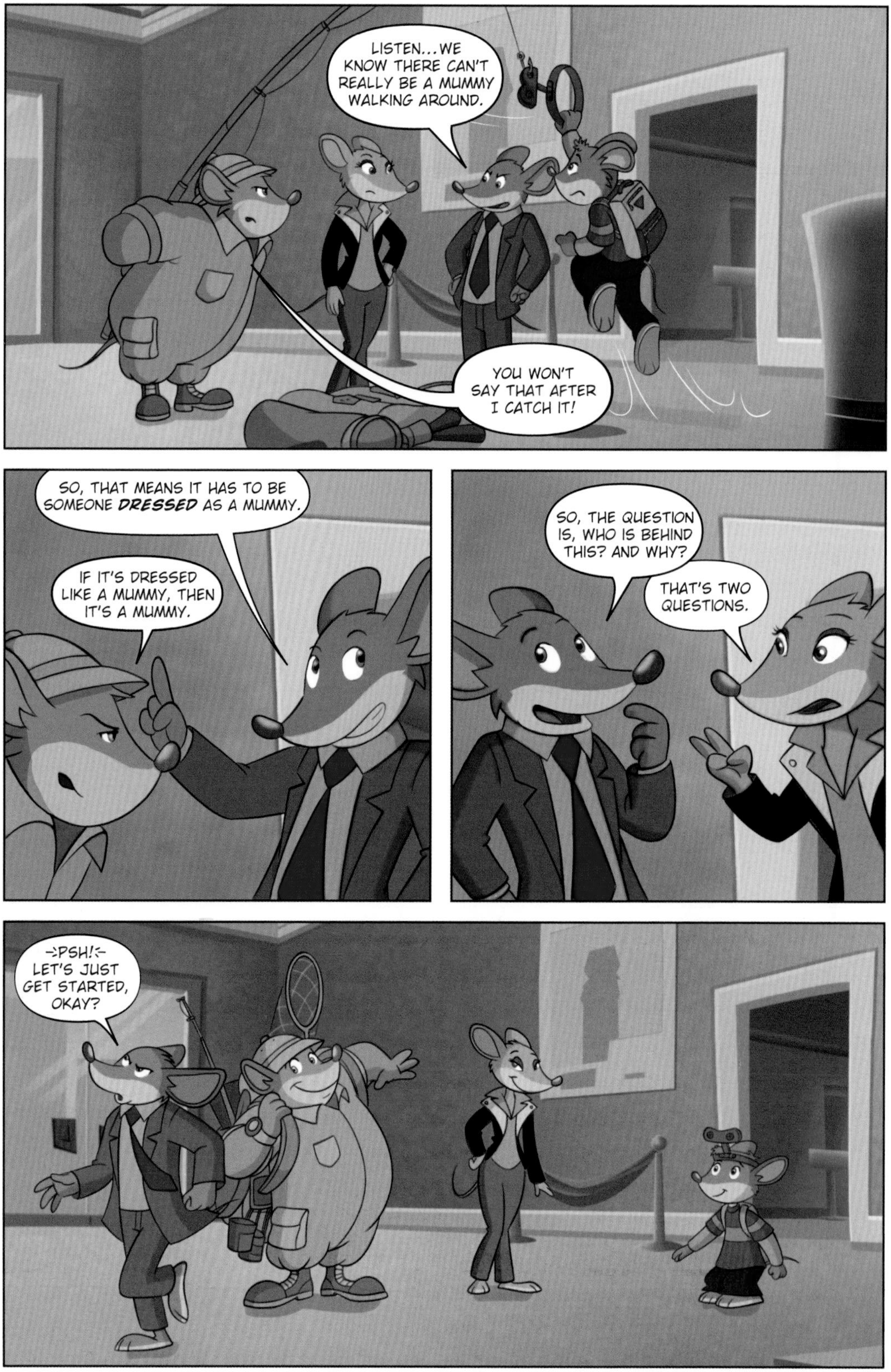
LISTEN...WE KNOW THERE CAN'T REALLY BE A MUMMY WALKING AROUND.
YOU WON'T SAY THAT AFTER I CATCH IT!
SO, THAT MEANS IT HAS TO BE SOMEONE DRESSED AS A MUMMY.
IF IT'S DRESSED LIKE A MUMMY, THEN IT'S A MUMMY.
SO, THE QUESTION IS, WHO IS BEHIND THIS? AND WHY?
THAT'S TWO QUESTIONS.
-PSH!- LET'S JUST GET STARTED, OKAY?

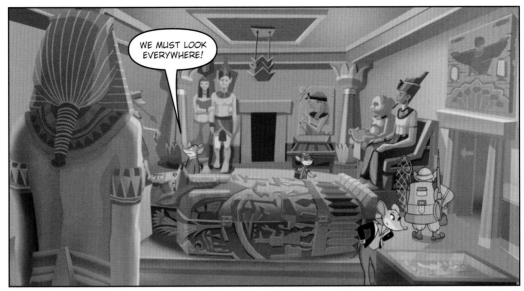

WE MUST LOOK EVERYWHERE!

THE SPECIAL *AKHENRATEN EXHIBIT* HAS BEEN DRAWING BIG CROWDS FOR WEEKS.

YOU MEAN PEOPLE COME TO THIS DUSTY PLACE ON PURPOSE?

ACHOO!

THIS PLACE *IS* DUSTY.

GESUNDHEIT, G!

THANKS, TRAP.

TRAP, WHAT ARE YOU DOING?

SCANNING FOR MUMMIES.

WITH A FISH FINDER?

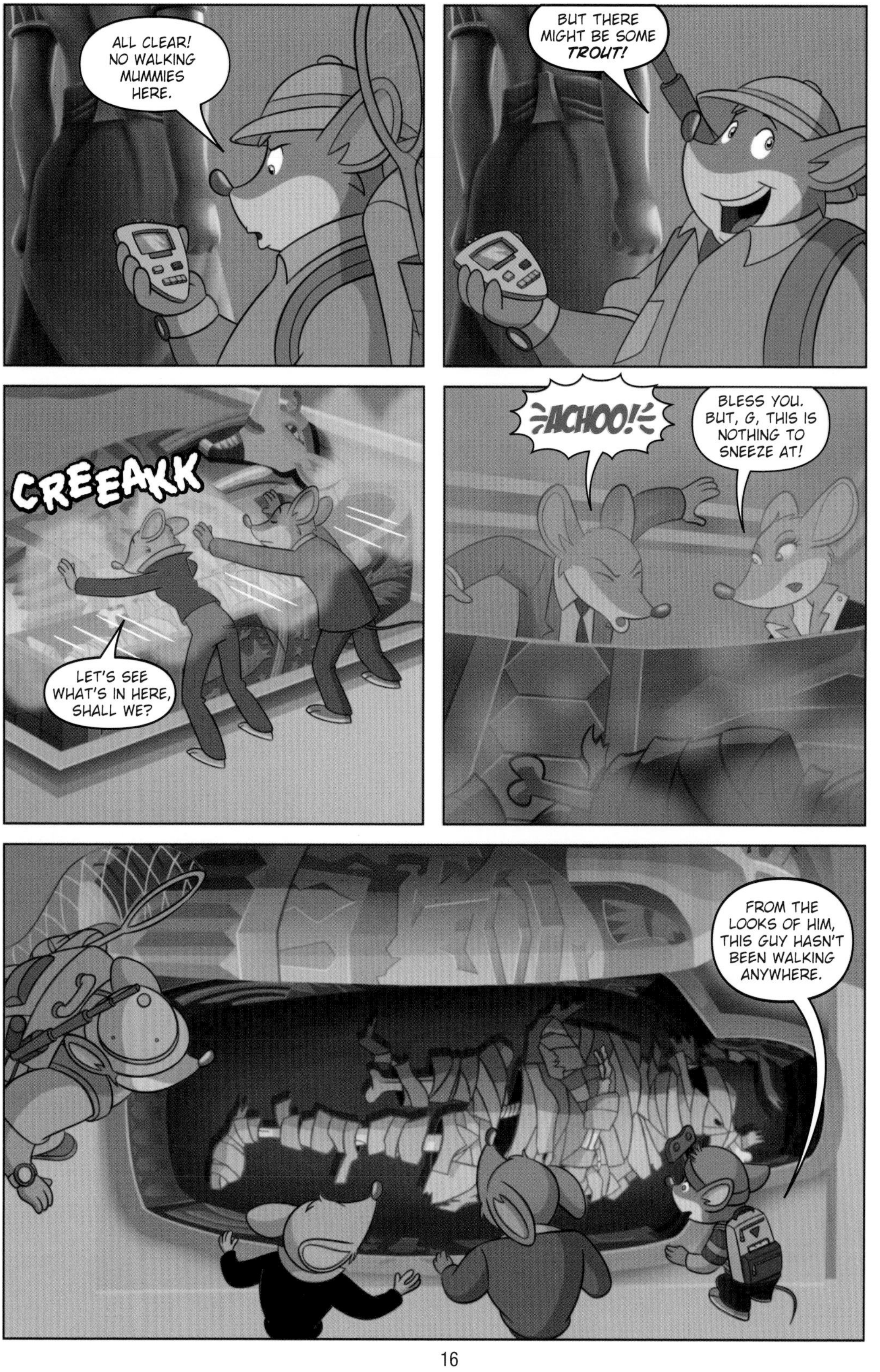
ALL CLEAR! NO WALKING MUMMIES HERE.
BUT THERE MIGHT BE SOME TROUT!
CREEAKK
LET'S SEE WHAT'S IN HERE, SHALL WE?
ACHOO!
BLESS YOU. BUT, G, THIS IS NOTHING TO SNEEZE AT!
FROM THE LOOKS OF HIM, THIS GUY HASN'T BEEN WALKING ANYWHERE.

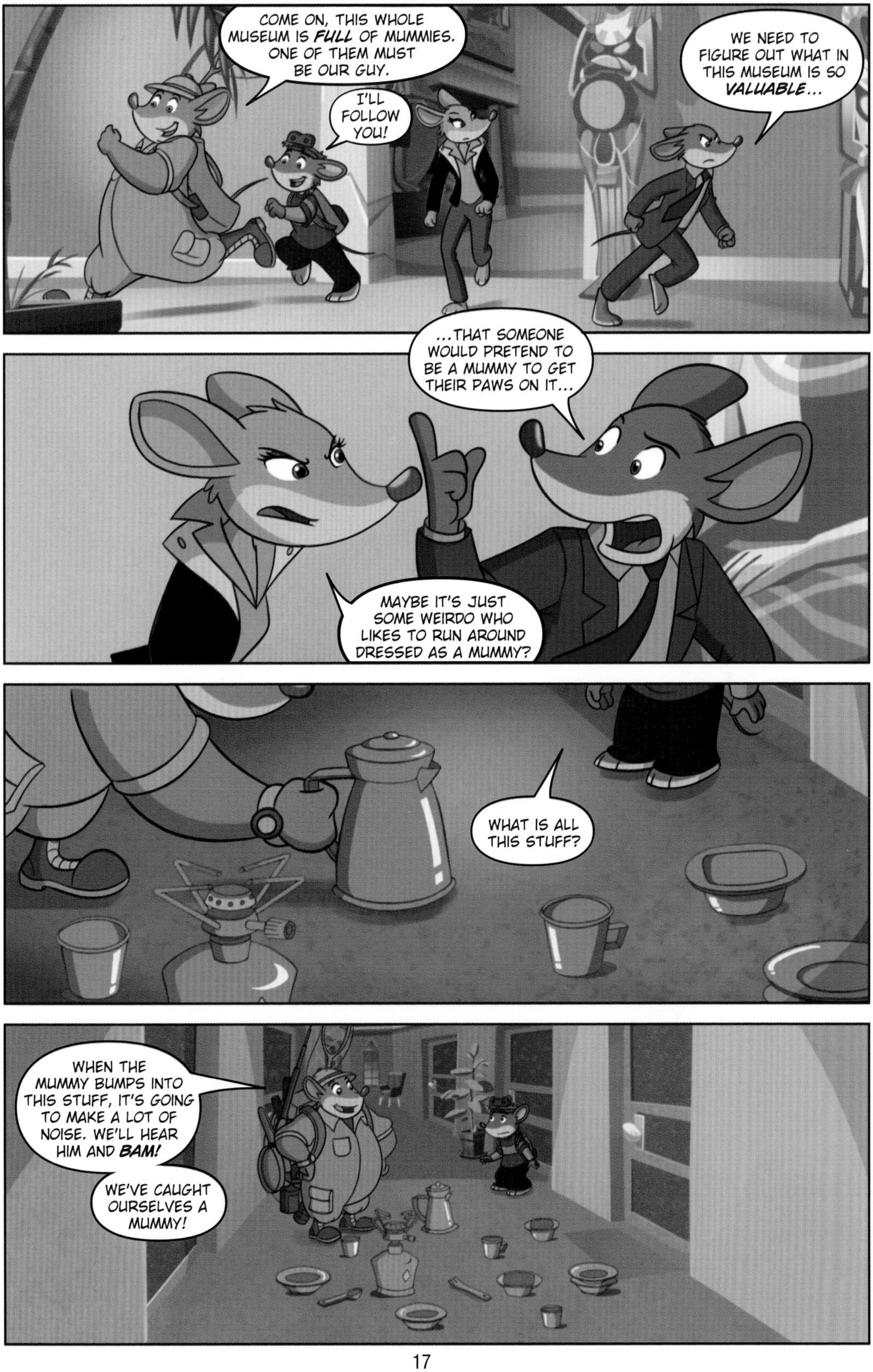
COME ON, THIS WHOLE MUSEUM IS ***FULL*** OF MUMMIES. ONE OF THEM MUST BE OUR GUY.
I'LL FOLLOW YOU!
WE NEED TO FIGURE OUT WHAT IN THIS MUSEUM IS SO ***VALUABLE***...
...THAT SOMEONE WOULD PRETEND TO BE A MUMMY TO GET THEIR PAWS ON IT...
MAYBE IT'S JUST SOME WEIRDO WHO LIKES TO RUN AROUND DRESSED AS A MUMMY?
WHAT IS ALL THIS STUFF?
WHEN THE MUMMY BUMPS INTO THIS STUFF, IT'S GOING TO MAKE A LOT OF NOISE. WE'LL HEAR HIM AND ***BAM!***
WE'VE CAUGHT OURSELVES A MUMMY!

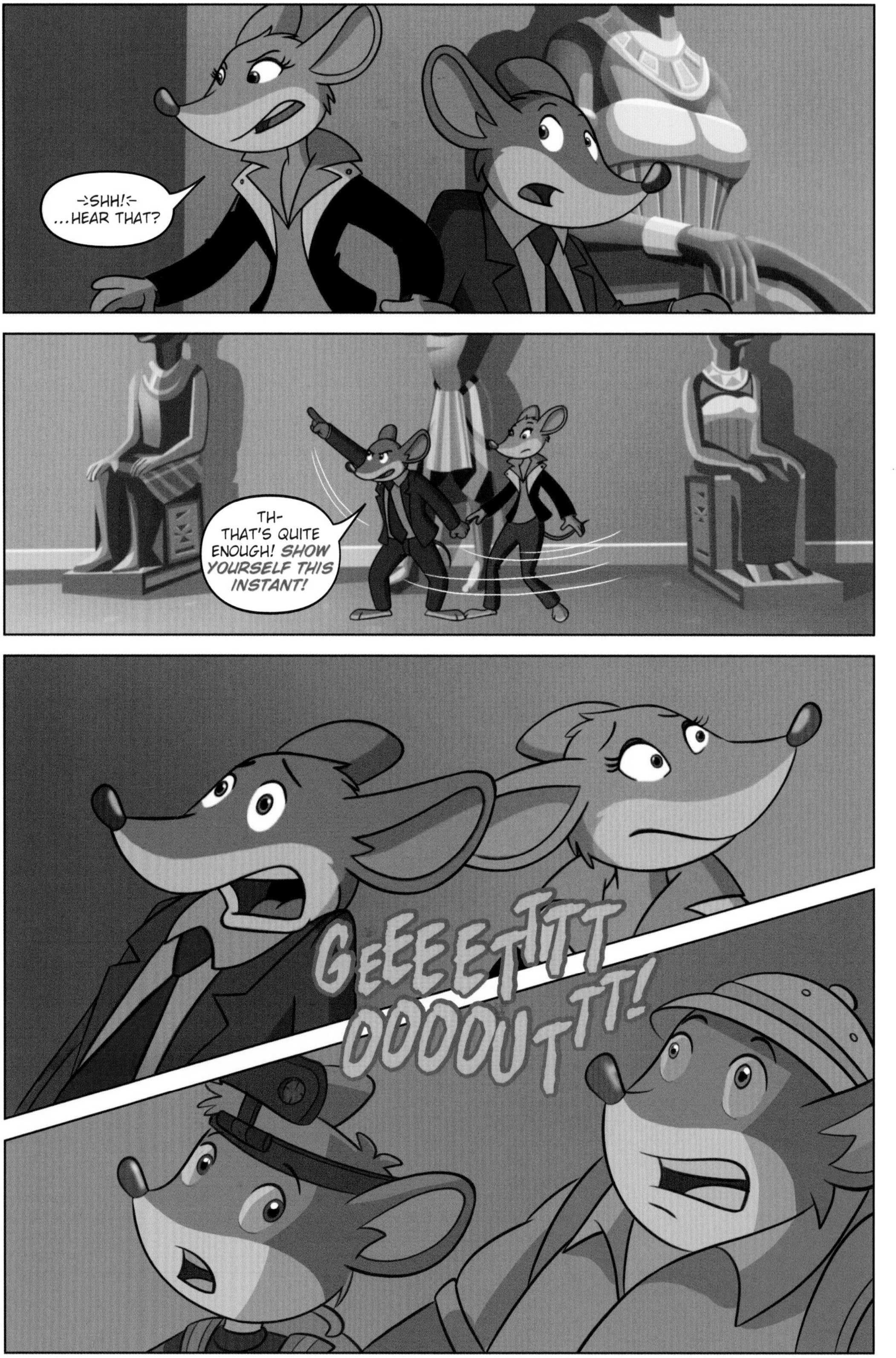

-SHH!- ...HEAR THAT?
TH- THAT'S QUITE ENOUGH! SHOW YOURSELF THIS INSTANT!
GEEEETTTT OOOOOUTTT!

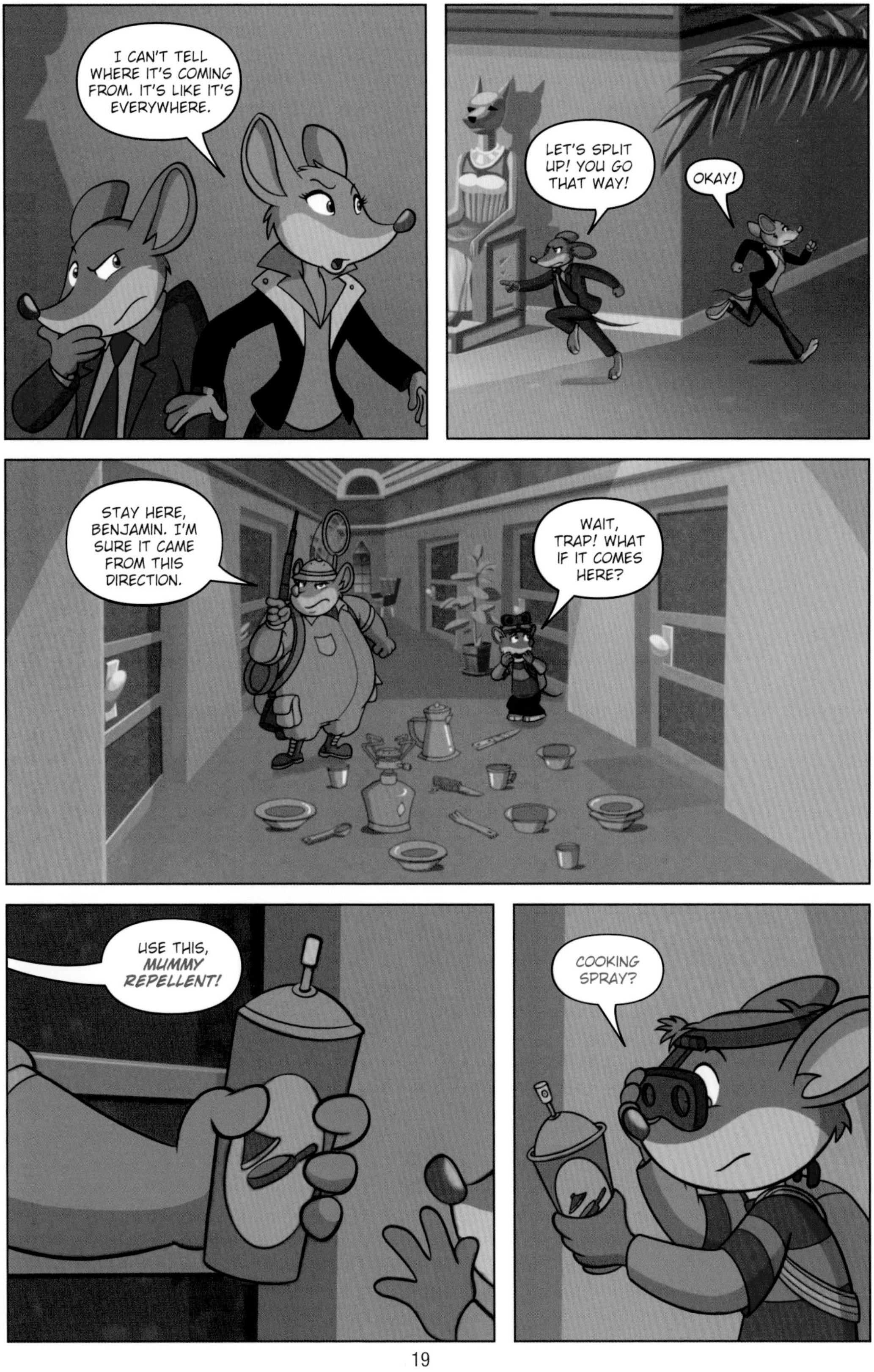
I CAN'T TELL WHERE IT'S COMING FROM. IT'S LIKE IT'S EVERYWHERE.
LET'S SPLIT UP! YOU GO THAT WAY!
OKAY!
STAY HERE, BENJAMIN. I'M SURE IT CAME FROM THIS DIRECTION.
WAIT, TRAP! WHAT IF IT COMES HERE?
USE THIS, *MUMMY REPELLENT!*
COOKING SPRAY?

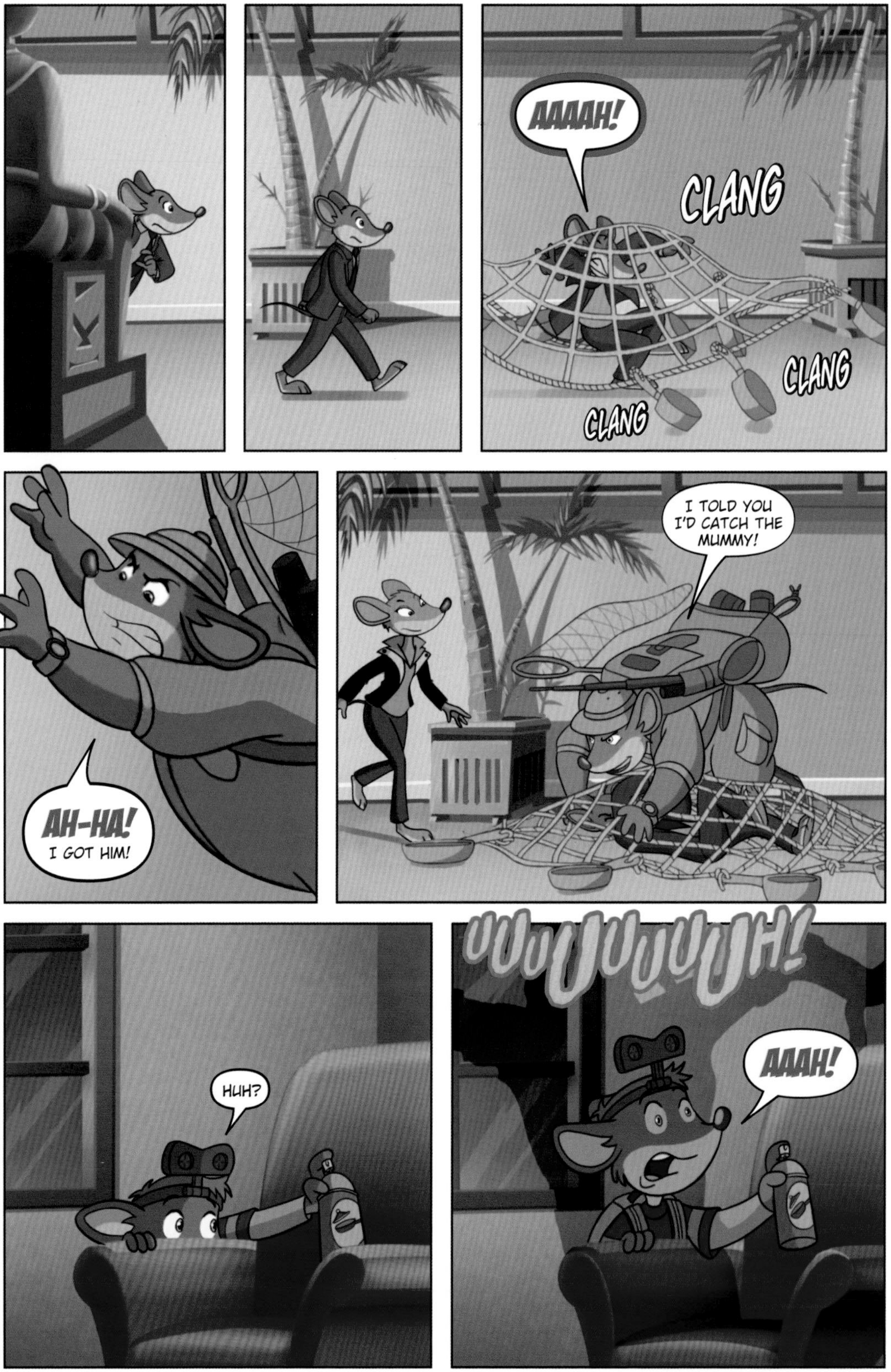
AAAAH!
CLANG
CLANG
CLANG
AH-HA!
I GOT HIM!
I TOLD YOU I'D CATCH THE MUMMY!
HUH?
UUUUUUUUUH!
AAAH!

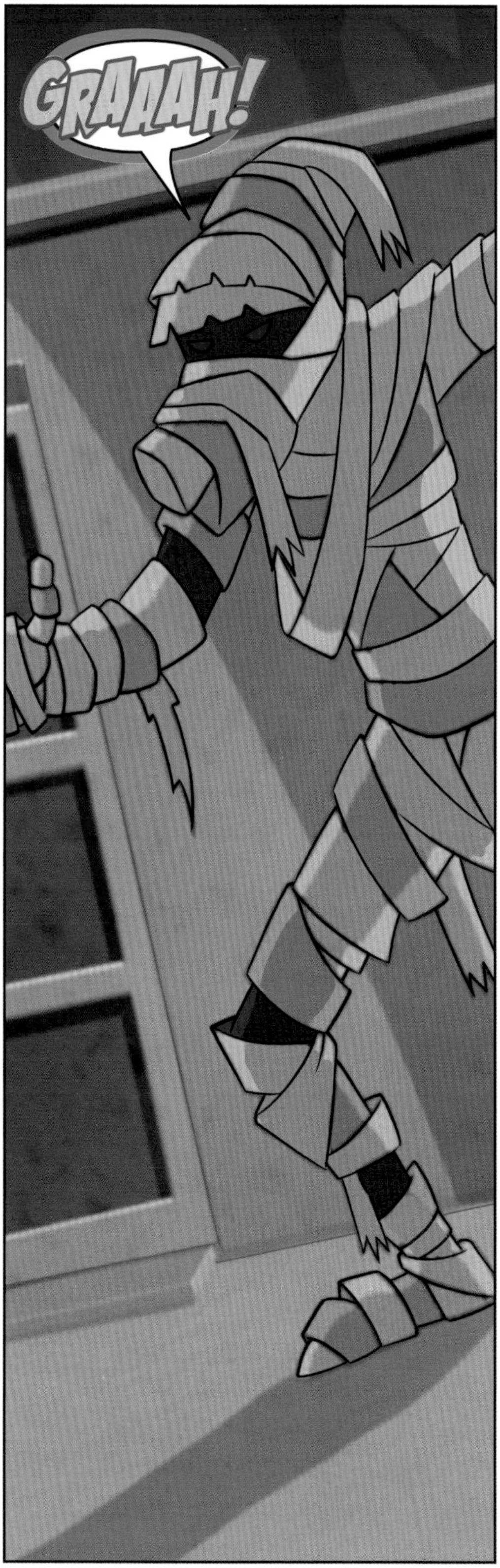
GRAAAH!

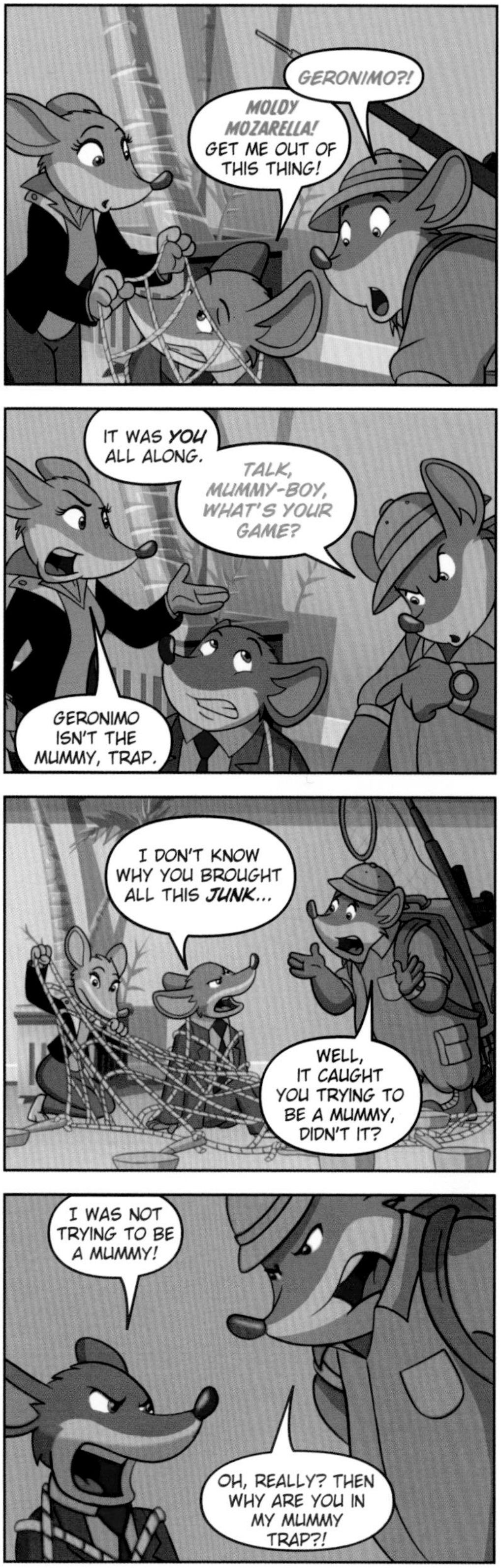
GERONIMO?!
MOLDY MOZARELLA! GET ME OUT OF THIS THING!
IT WAS YOU ALL ALONG.
TALK, MUMMY-BOY, WHAT'S YOUR GAME?
GERONIMO ISN'T THE MUMMY, TRAP.
I DON'T KNOW WHY YOU BROUGHT ALL THIS JUNK...
WELL, IT CAUGHT YOU TRYING TO BE A MUMMY, DIDN'T IT?
I WAS NOT TRYING TO BE A MUMMY!
OH, REALLY? THEN WHY ARE YOU IN MY MUMMY TRAP?!

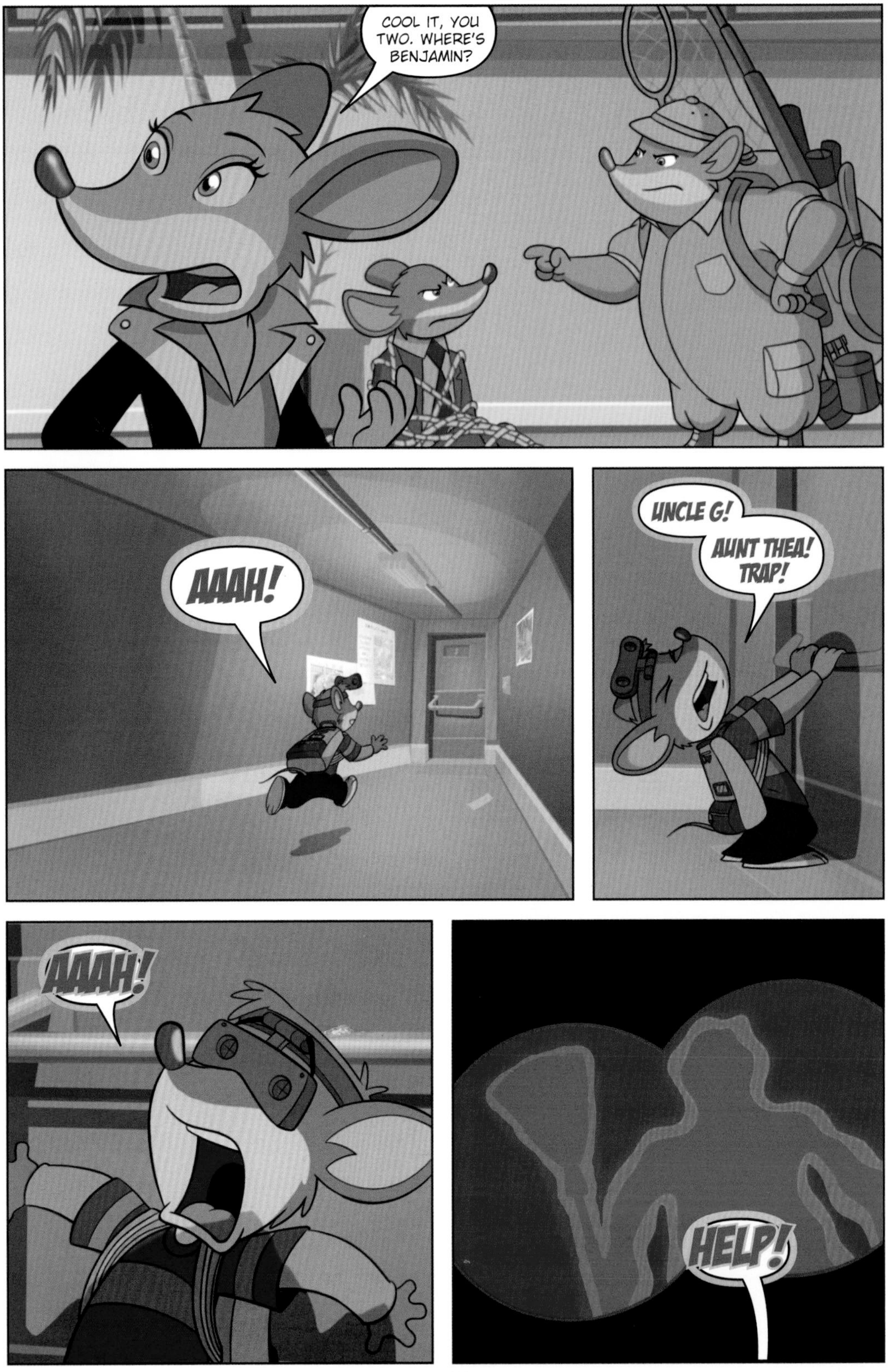

COOL IT, YOU TWO. WHERE'S BENJAMIN?
AAAH!
UNCLE G!
AUNT THEA! TRAP!
AAAH!
HELP!

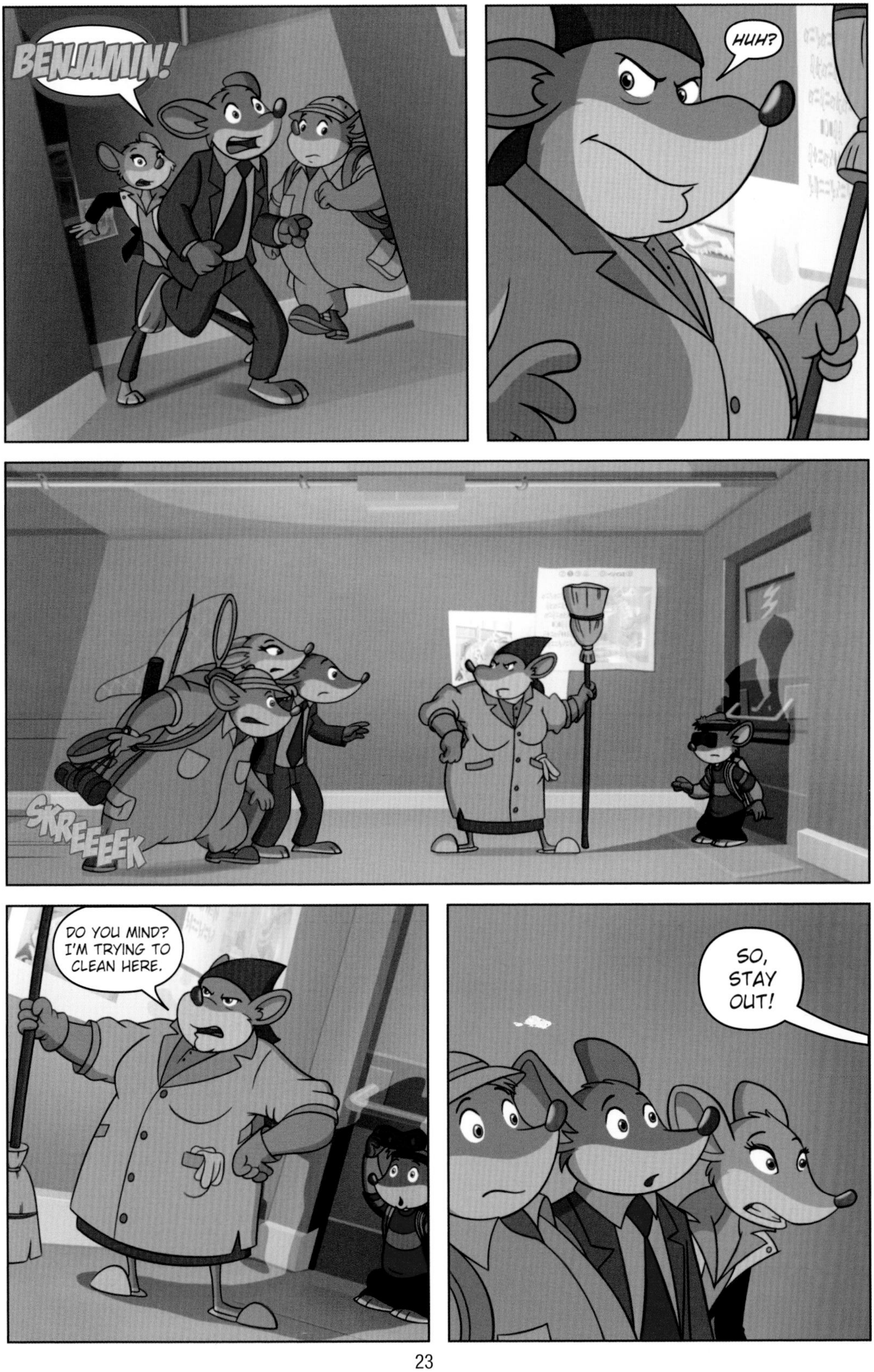
BENJAMIN!
HUH?
SKREEEEK
DO YOU MIND? I'M TRYING TO CLEAN HERE.
SO, STAY OUT!

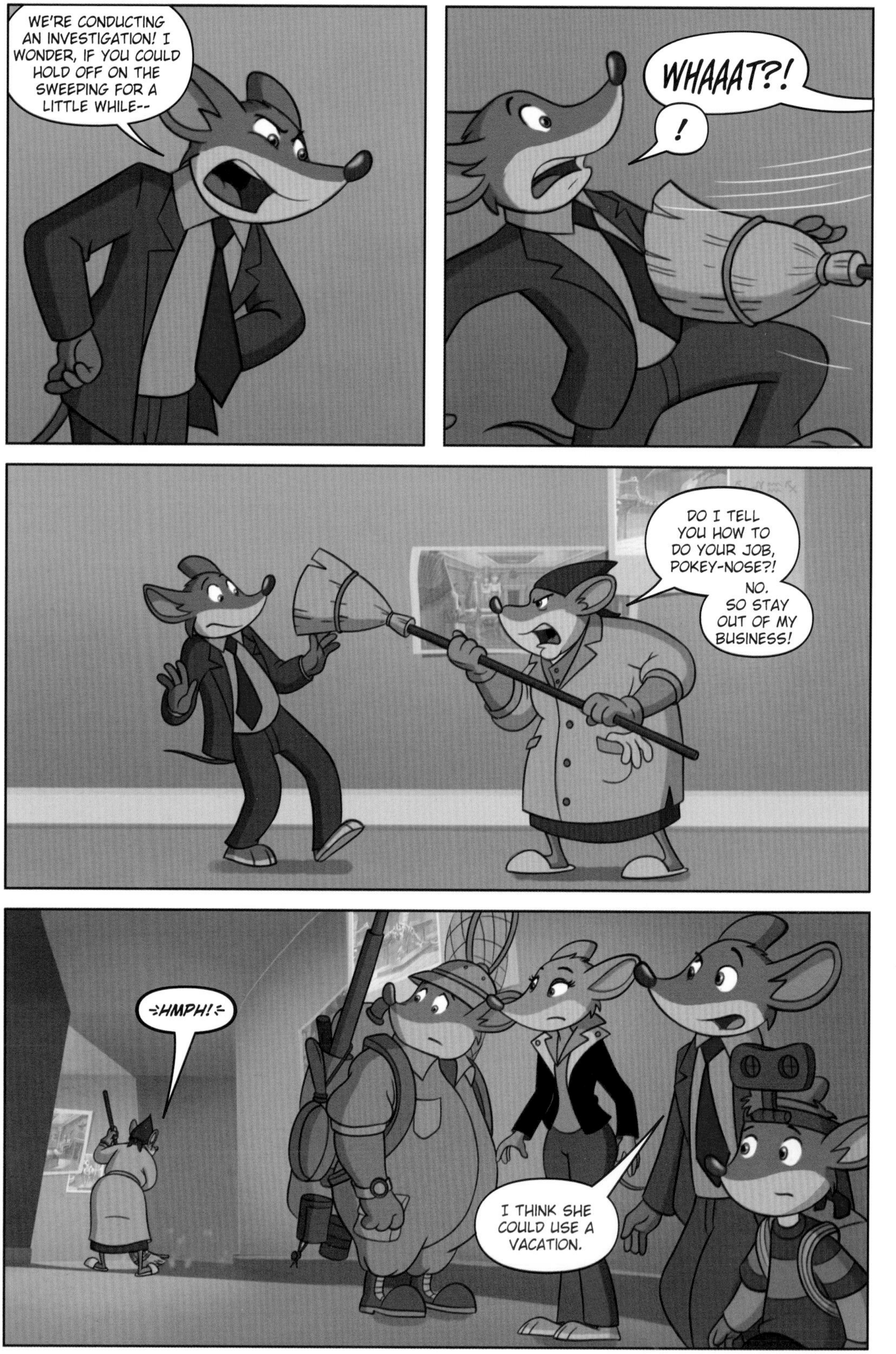
WE'RE CONDUCTING AN INVESTIGATION! I WONDER, IF YOU COULD HOLD OFF ON THE SWEEPING FOR A LITTLE WHILE--
WHAAAT?!
!
DO I TELL YOU HOW TO DO YOUR JOB, POKEY-NOSE?!
NO. SO STAY OUT OF MY BUSINESS!
HMPH!
I THINK SHE COULD USE A VACATION.

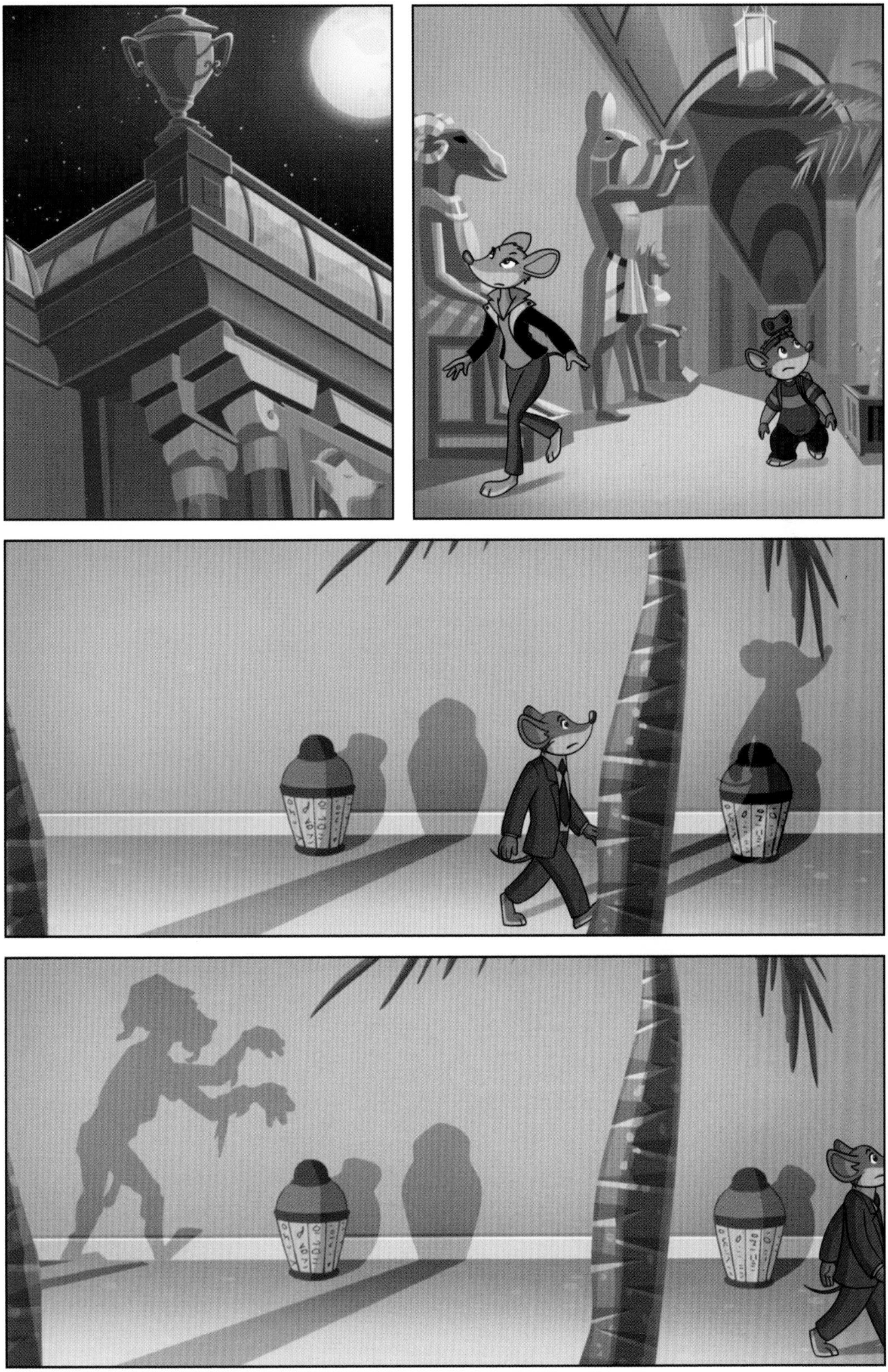

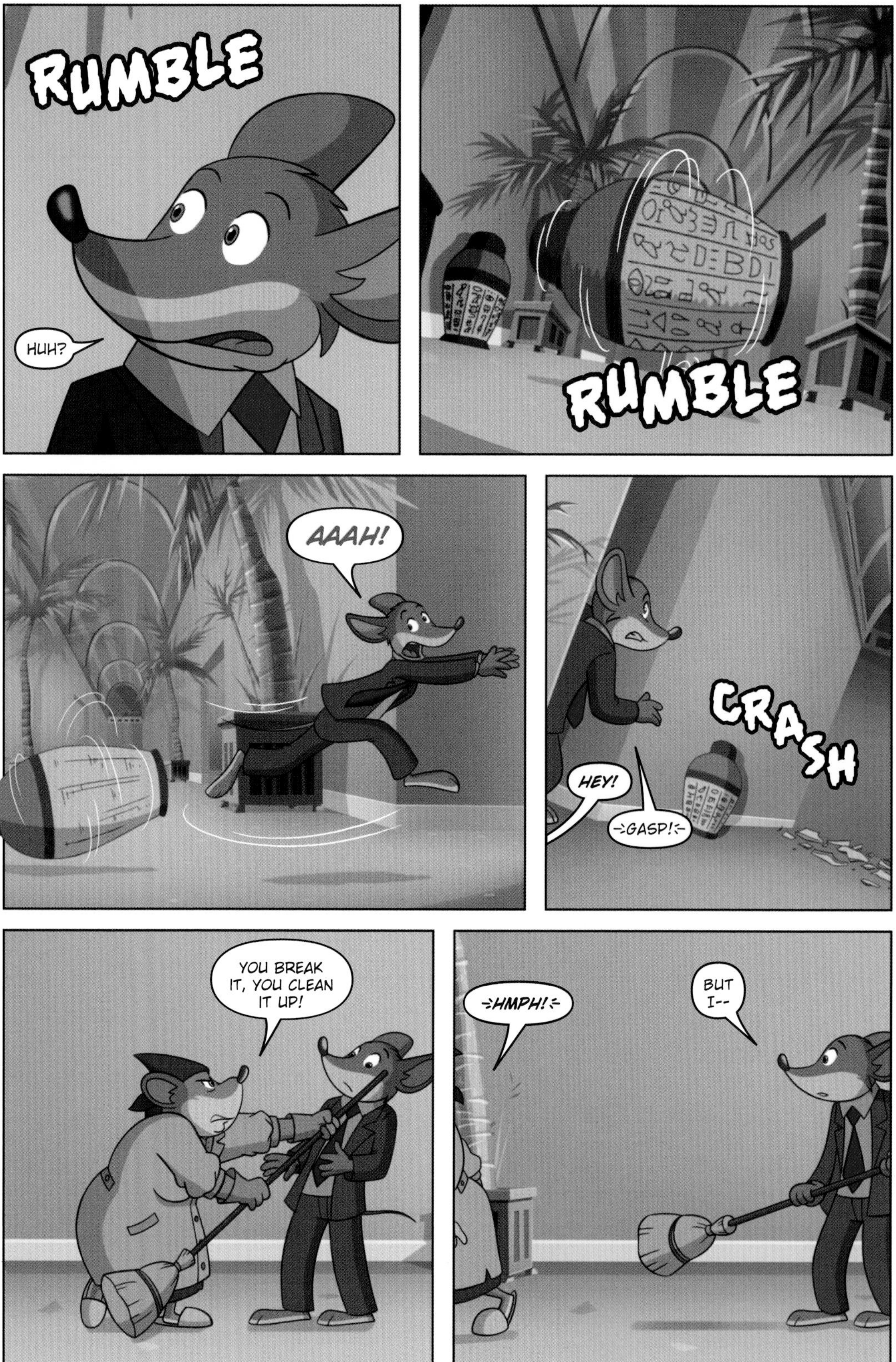
RUMBLE
HUH?
RUMBLE
AAAH!
CRASH
HEY!
GASP!
YOU BREAK IT, YOU CLEAN IT UP!
HMPH!
BUT I--

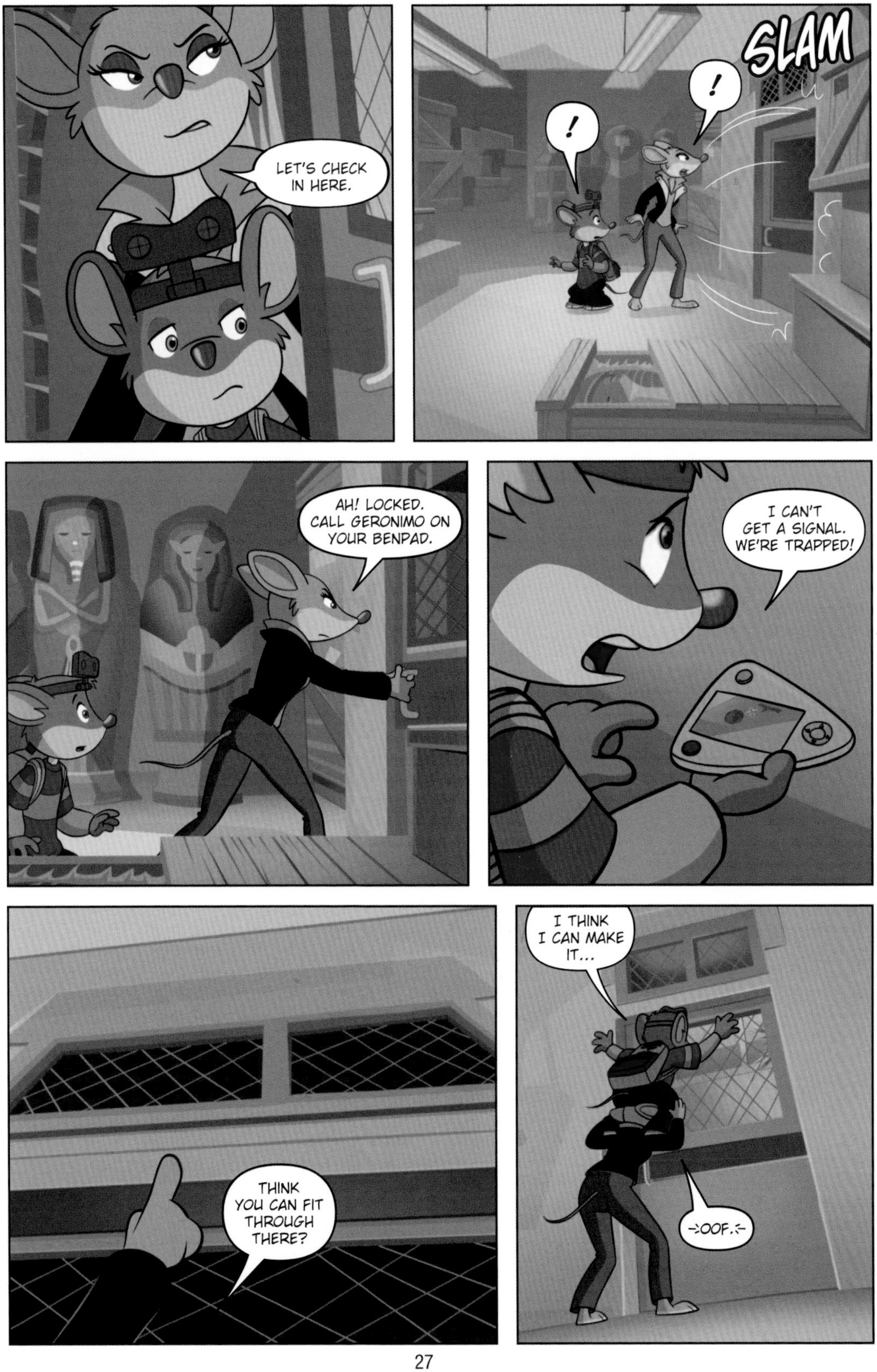
LET'S CHECK IN HERE.
SLAM
!
!
AH! LOCKED. CALL GERONIMO ON YOUR BENPAD.
I CAN'T GET A SIGNAL. WE'RE TRAPPED!
THINK YOU CAN FIT THROUGH THERE?
I THINK I CAN MAKE IT...
OOF.

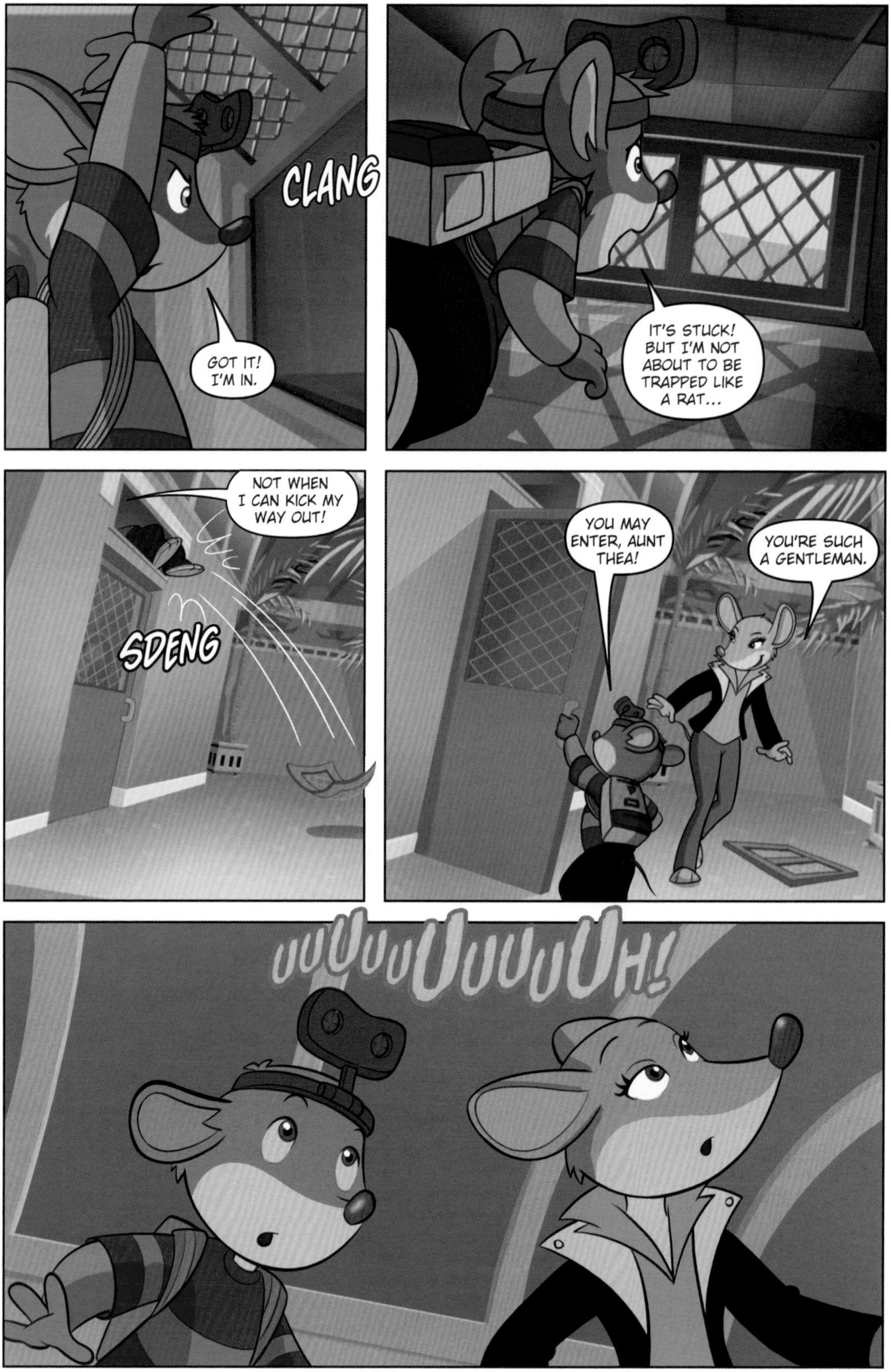
CLANG
GOT IT! I'M IN.
IT'S STUCK! BUT I'M NOT ABOUT TO BE TRAPPED LIKE A RAT...
NOT WHEN I CAN KICK MY WAY OUT!
SDENG
YOU MAY ENTER, AUNT THEA!
YOU'RE SUCH A GENTLEMAN.
UUUUUUUUUUUUH!

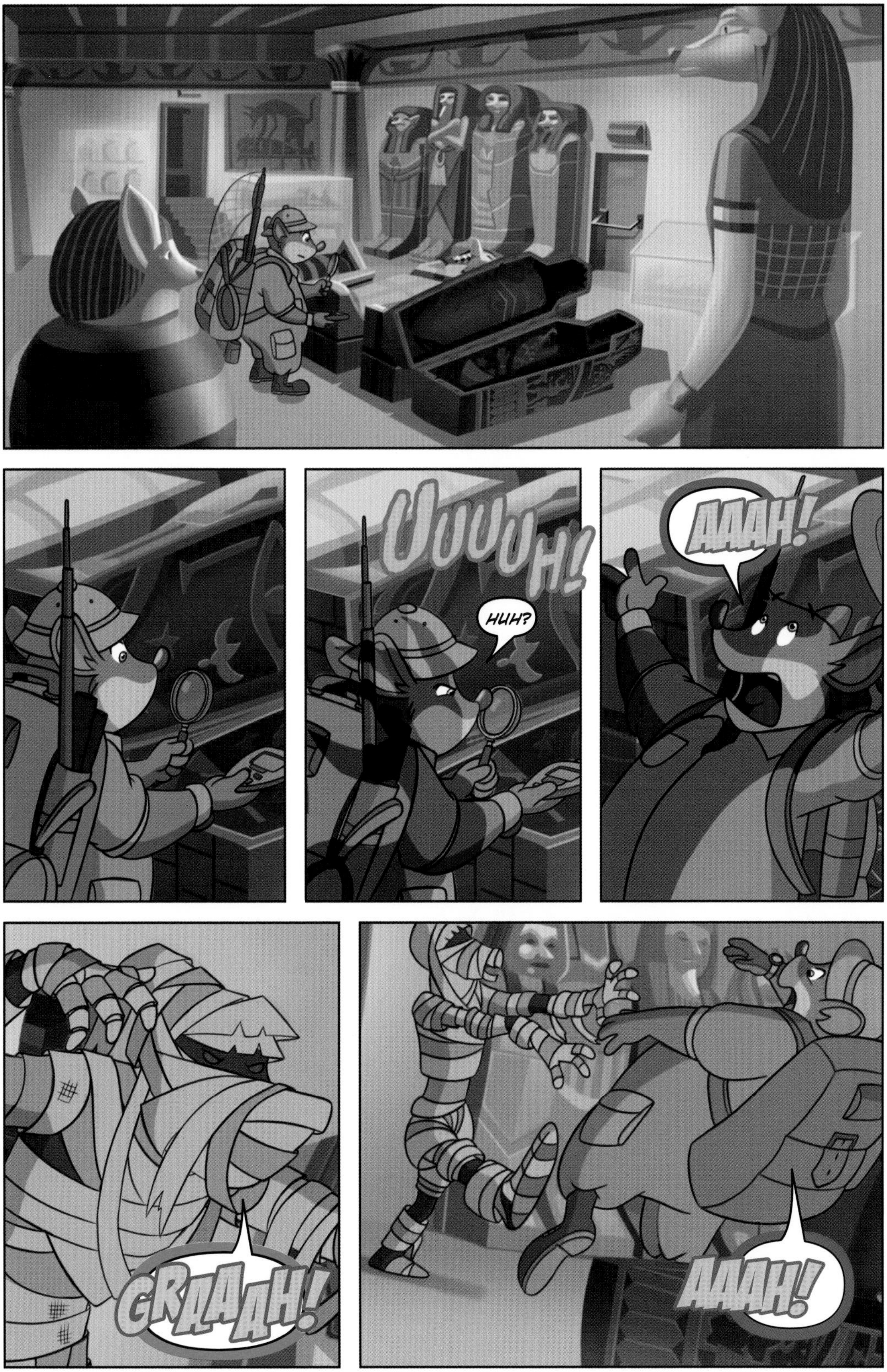
UUUUH!
HUH?
AAAH!
GRAAAH!
AAAH!

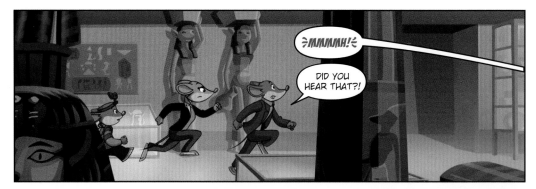

≳MMMMH!≲

DID YOU HEAR THAT?!

OH, NO! LOOK!

RATTLE

RATTLE

LET'S SEE WHAT'S IN HERE.

RATTLE

RATTLE

≳MMMMH!≲

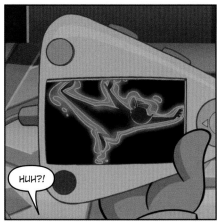

HUH?!

LET'S FIND OUT THE OLD-FASHIONED WAY... ACTUALLY LOOKING INSIDE!

≳UNFF!≲

IT WAS THE MUMMY! I SAW IT!

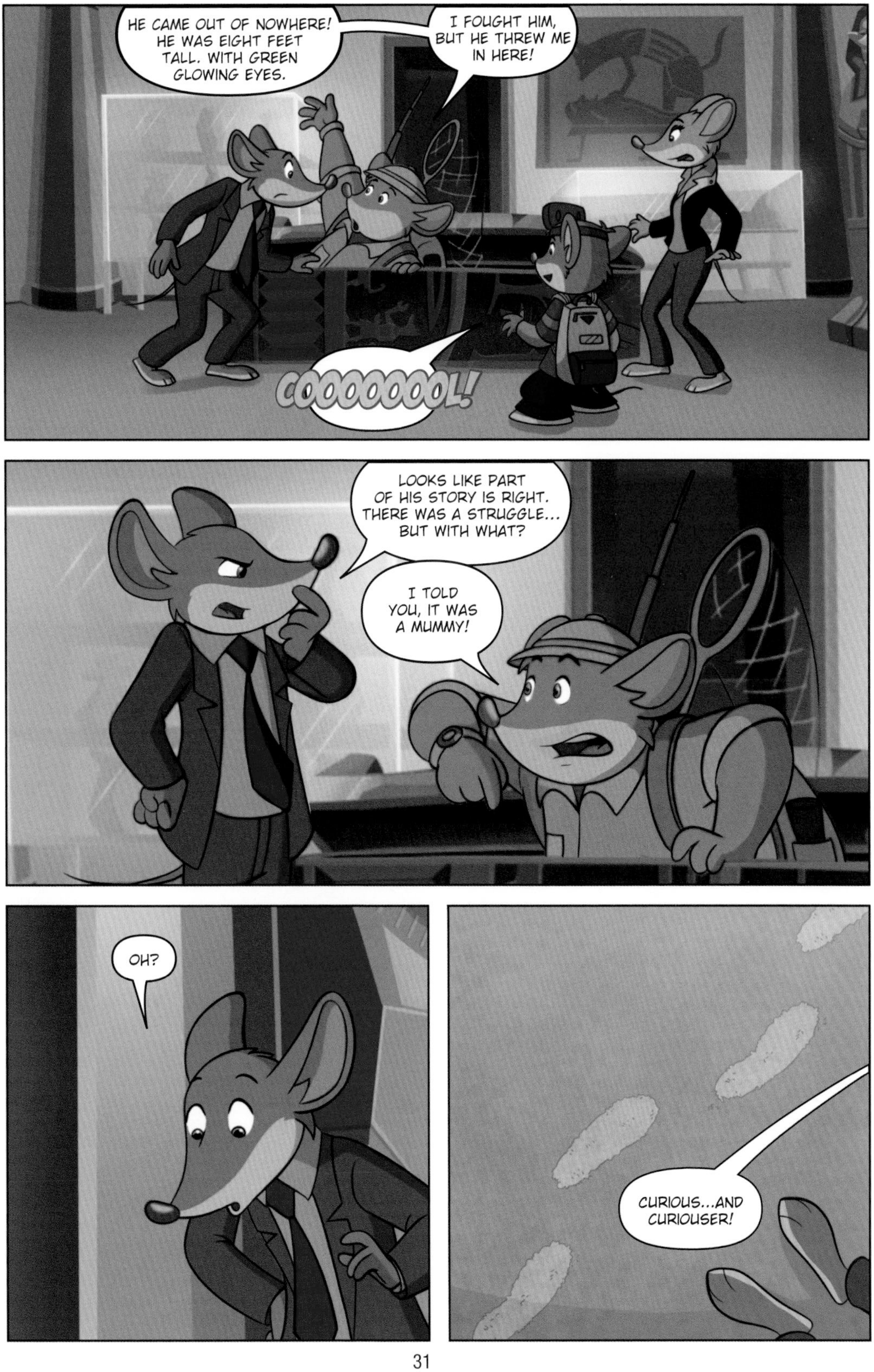
HE CAME OUT OF NOWHERE! HE WAS EIGHT FEET TALL. WITH GREEN GLOWING EYES.
I FOUGHT HIM, BUT HE THREW ME IN HERE!
COOOOOOOL!
LOOKS LIKE PART OF HIS STORY IS RIGHT. THERE WAS A STRUGGLE... BUT WITH WHAT?
I TOLD YOU, IT WAS A MUMMY!
OH?
CURIOUS...AND CURIOUSER!

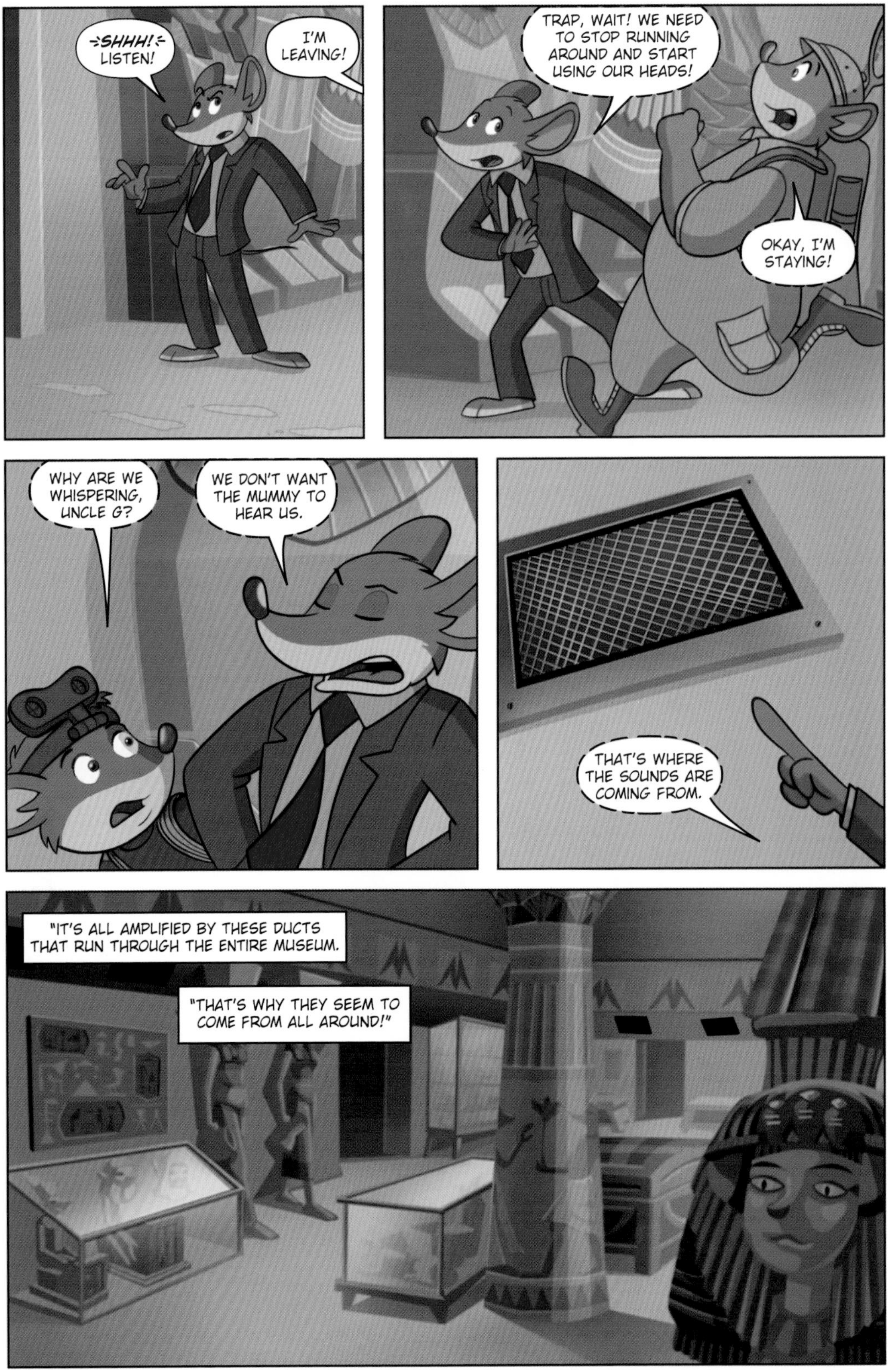

SHHH!
LISTEN!
I'M LEAVING!
TRAP, WAIT! WE NEED TO STOP RUNNING AROUND AND START USING OUR HEADS!
OKAY, I'M STAYING!
WHY ARE WE WHISPERING, UNCLE G?
WE DON'T WANT THE MUMMY TO HEAR US.
THAT'S WHERE THE SOUNDS ARE COMING FROM.
"IT'S ALL AMPLIFIED BY THESE DUCTS THAT RUN THROUGH THE ENTIRE MUSEUM.
"THAT'S WHY THEY SEEM TO COME FROM ALL AROUND!"

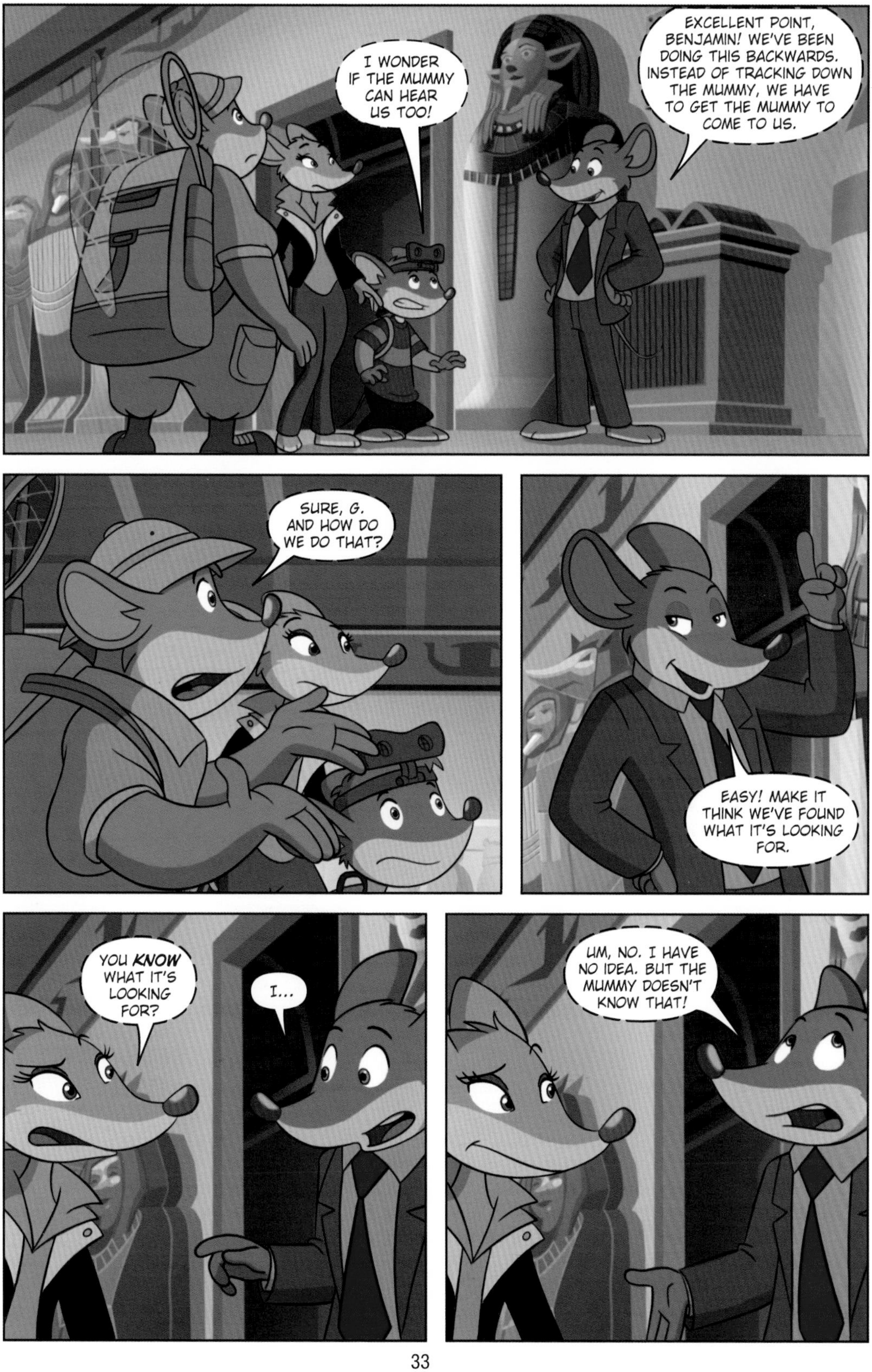
I WONDER IF THE MUMMY CAN HEAR US TOO!
EXCELLENT POINT, BENJAMIN! WE'VE BEEN DOING THIS BACKWARDS. INSTEAD OF TRACKING DOWN THE MUMMY, WE HAVE TO GET THE MUMMY TO COME TO US.
SURE, G. AND HOW DO WE DO THAT?
EASY! MAKE IT THINK WE'VE FOUND WHAT IT'S LOOKING FOR.
YOU **KNOW** WHAT IT'S LOOKING FOR?
I...
UM, NO. I HAVE NO IDEA. BUT THE MUMMY DOESN'T KNOW THAT!

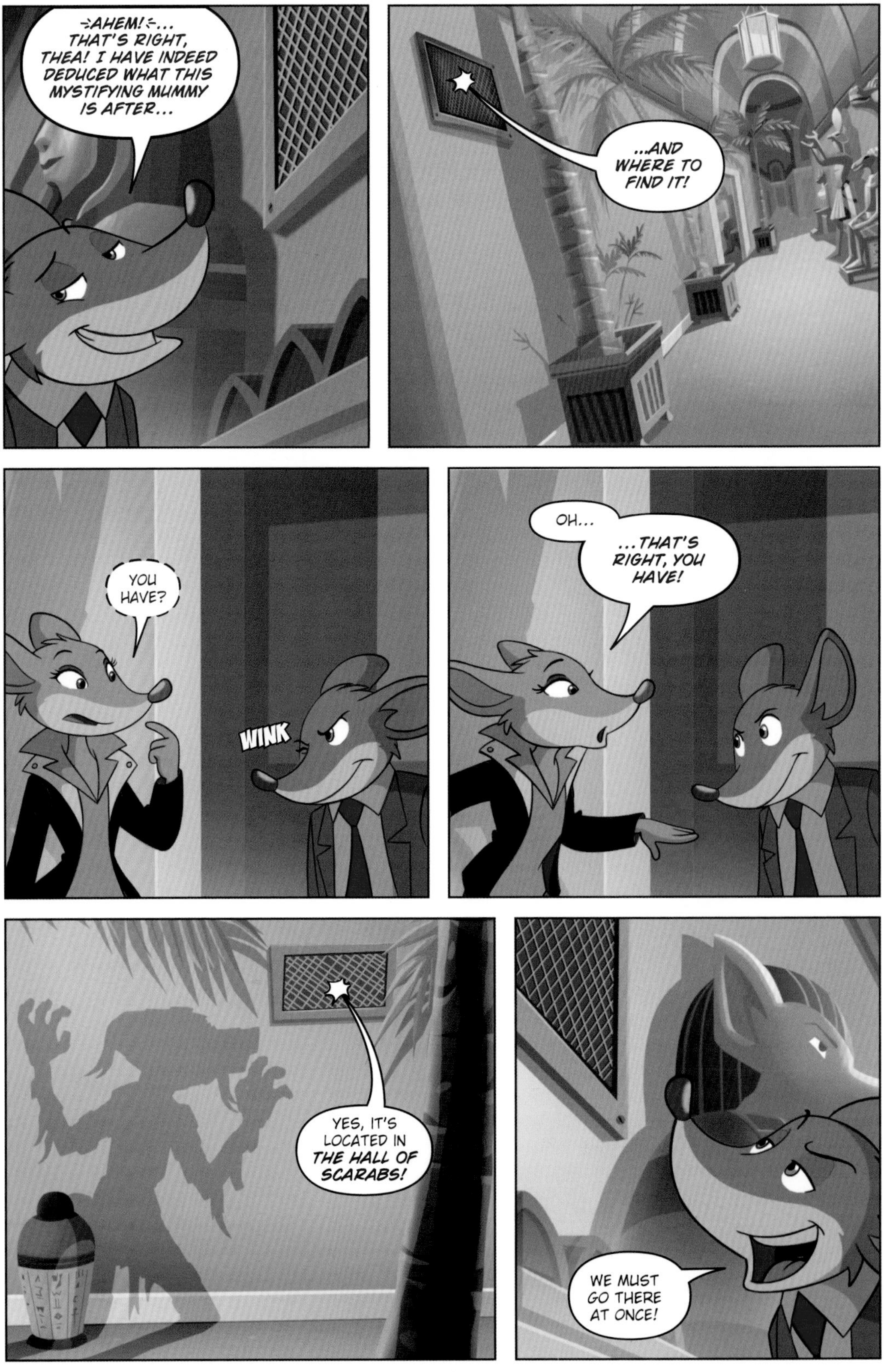

-AHEM!-... THAT'S RIGHT, THEA! I HAVE INDEED DEDUCED WHAT THIS MYSTIFYING MUMMY IS AFTER...
...AND WHERE TO FIND IT!
YOU HAVE?
WINK
OH...
...THAT'S RIGHT, YOU HAVE!
YES, IT'S LOCATED IN THE HALL OF SCARABS!
WE MUST GO THERE AT ONCE!

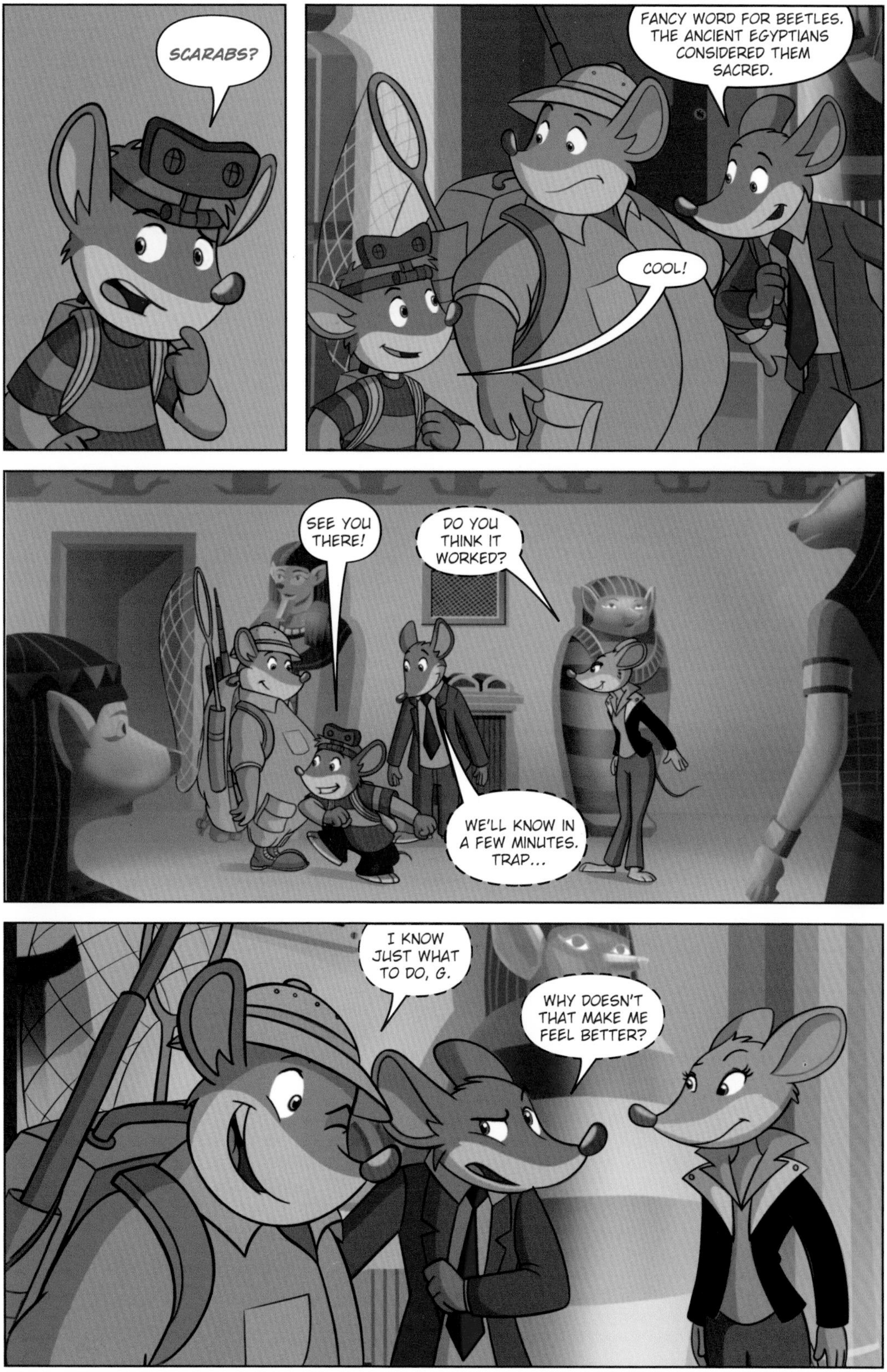
SCARABS?
FANCY WORD FOR BEETLES. THE ANCIENT EGYPTIANS CONSIDERED THEM SACRED.
COOL!
SEE YOU THERE!
DO YOU THINK IT WORKED?
WE'LL KNOW IN A FEW MINUTES. TRAP...
I KNOW JUST WHAT TO DO, G.
WHY DOESN'T THAT MAKE ME FEEL BETTER?

UUUUUUUUH!

OH!

CRAAAH!

CRAAAH!

OH, NOOO! A MUMMYYY!

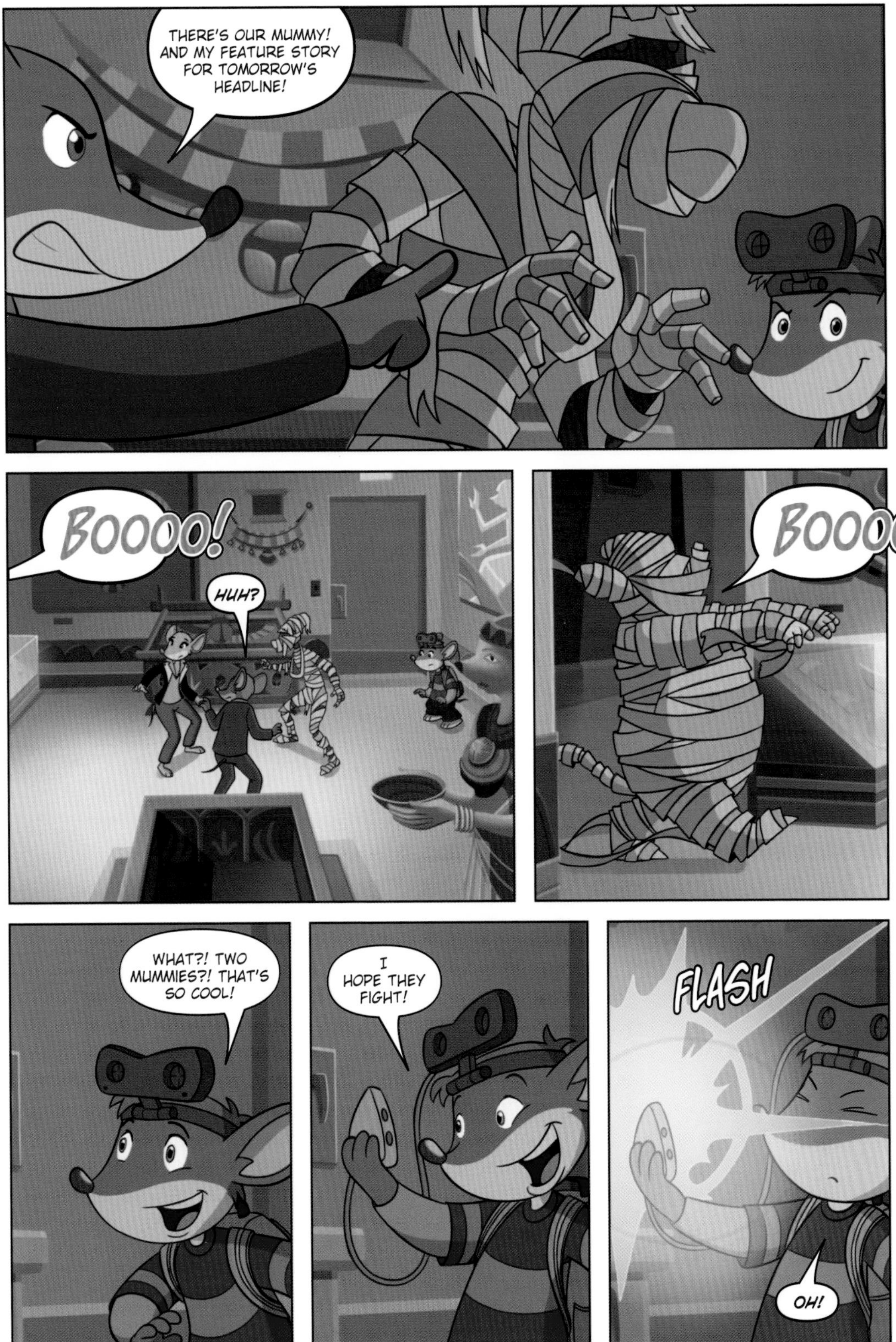
THERE'S OUR MUMMY! AND MY FEATURE STORY FOR TOMORROW'S HEADLINE!
BOOOO!
HUH?
BOOOO!
WHAT?! TWO MUMMIES?! THAT'S SO COOL!
I HOPE THEY FIGHT!
FLASH
OH!

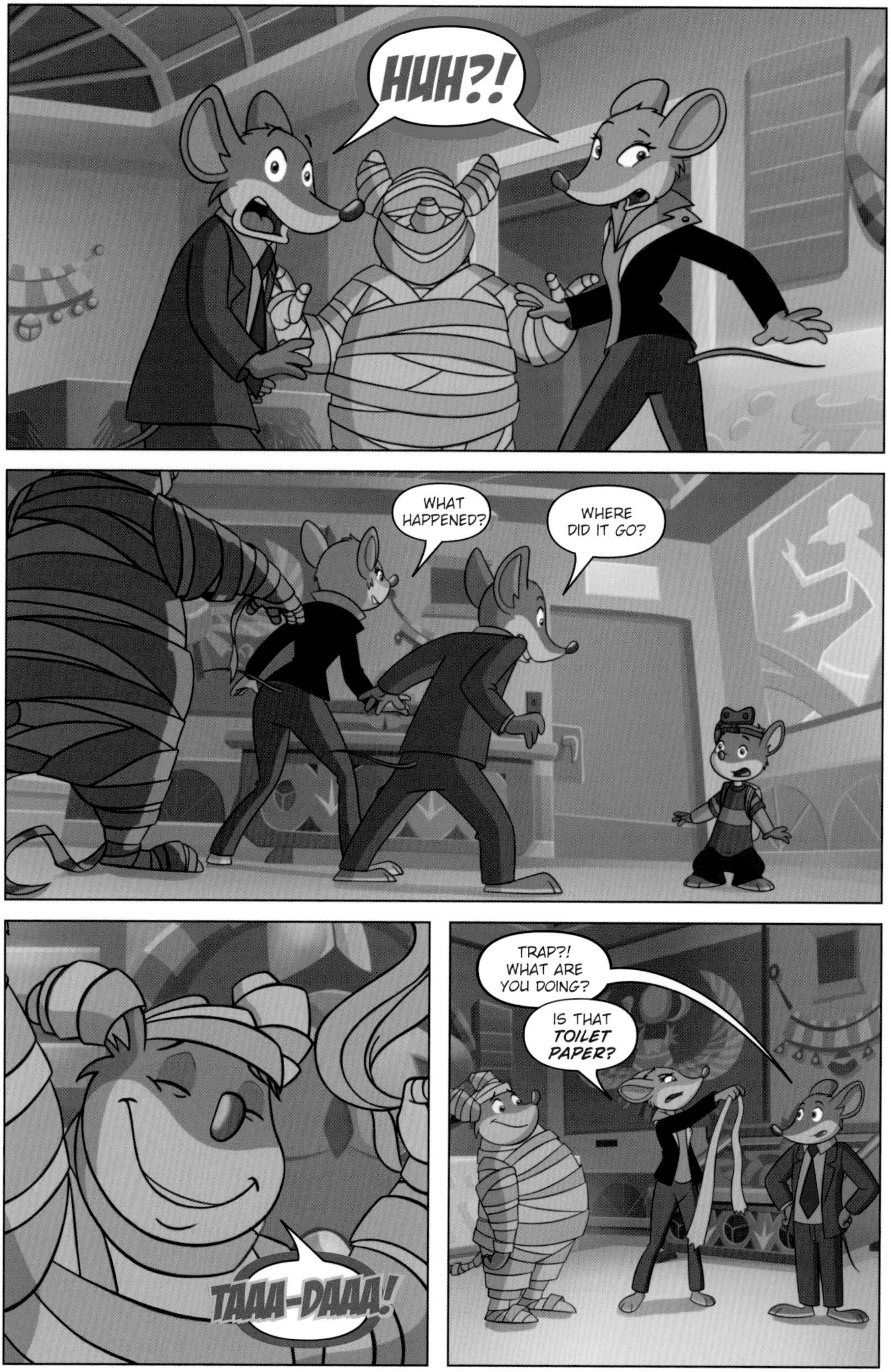
HUH?!
WHAT HAPPENED?
WHERE DID IT GO?
TAAA-DAAA!
TRAP?! WHAT ARE YOU DOING?
IS THAT *TOILET PAPER?*

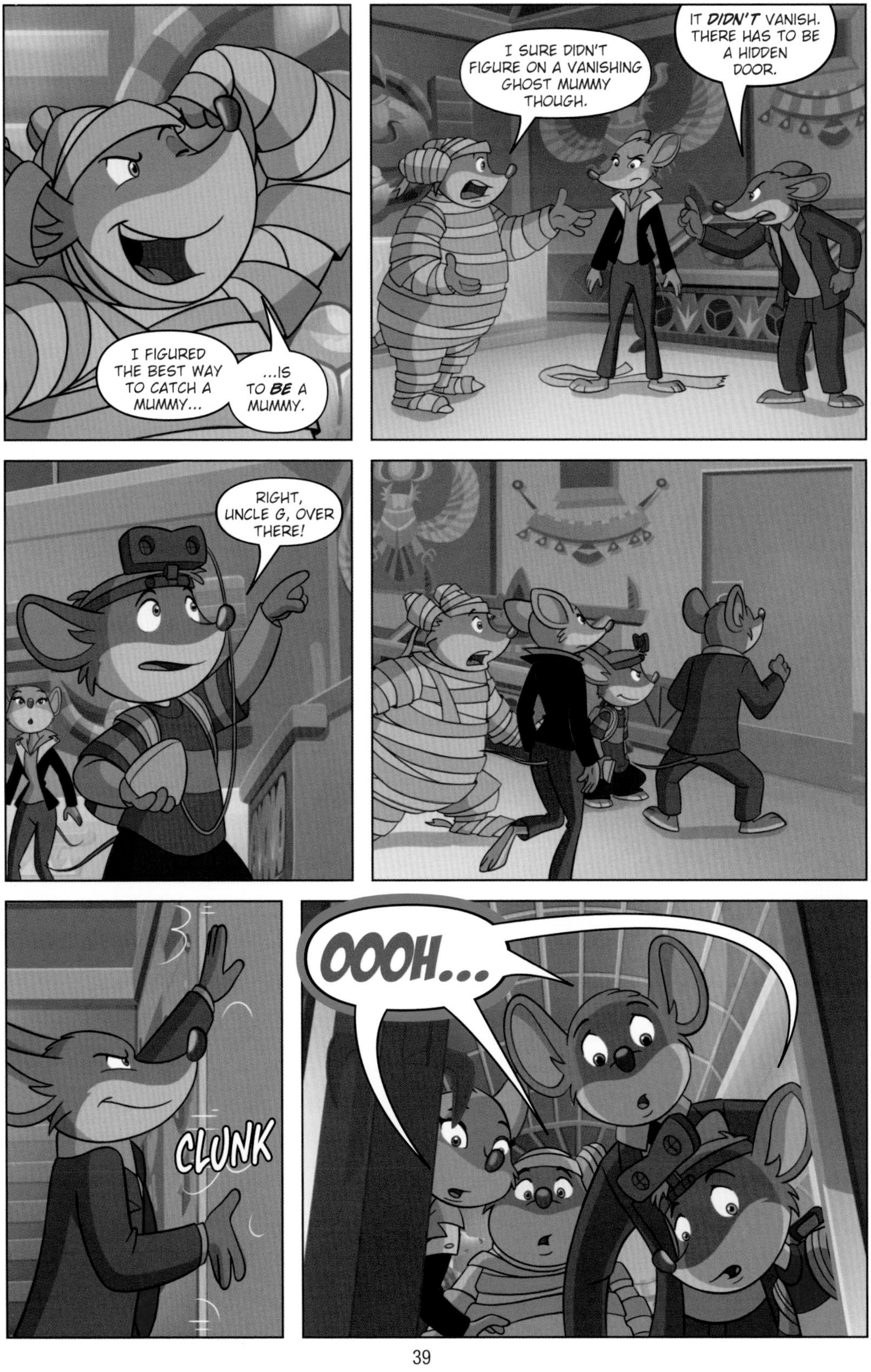
I FIGURED THE BEST WAY TO CATCH A MUMMY...
...IS TO *BE* A MUMMY.
I SURE DIDN'T FIGURE ON A VANISHING GHOST MUMMY THOUGH.
IT *DIDN'T* VANISH. THERE HAS TO BE A HIDDEN DOOR.
RIGHT, UNCLE G, OVER THERE!
CLUNK
OOOH...

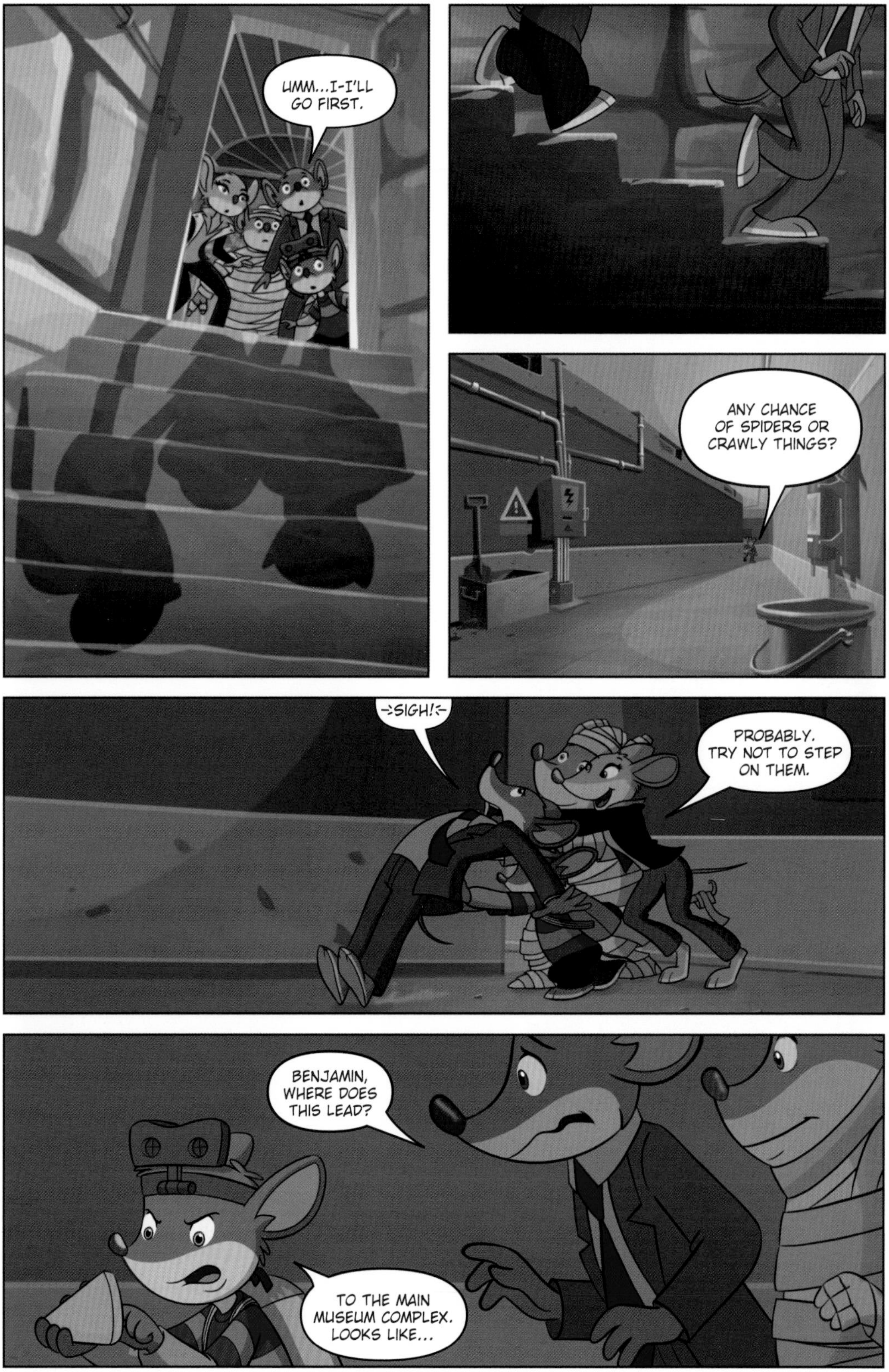
UMM...I-I'LL GO FIRST.
ANY CHANCE OF SPIDERS OR CRAWLY THINGS?
-SIGH!-
PROBABLY. TRY NOT TO STEP ON THEM.
BENJAMIN, WHERE DOES THIS LEAD?
TO THE MAIN MUSEUM COMPLEX. LOOKS LIKE...

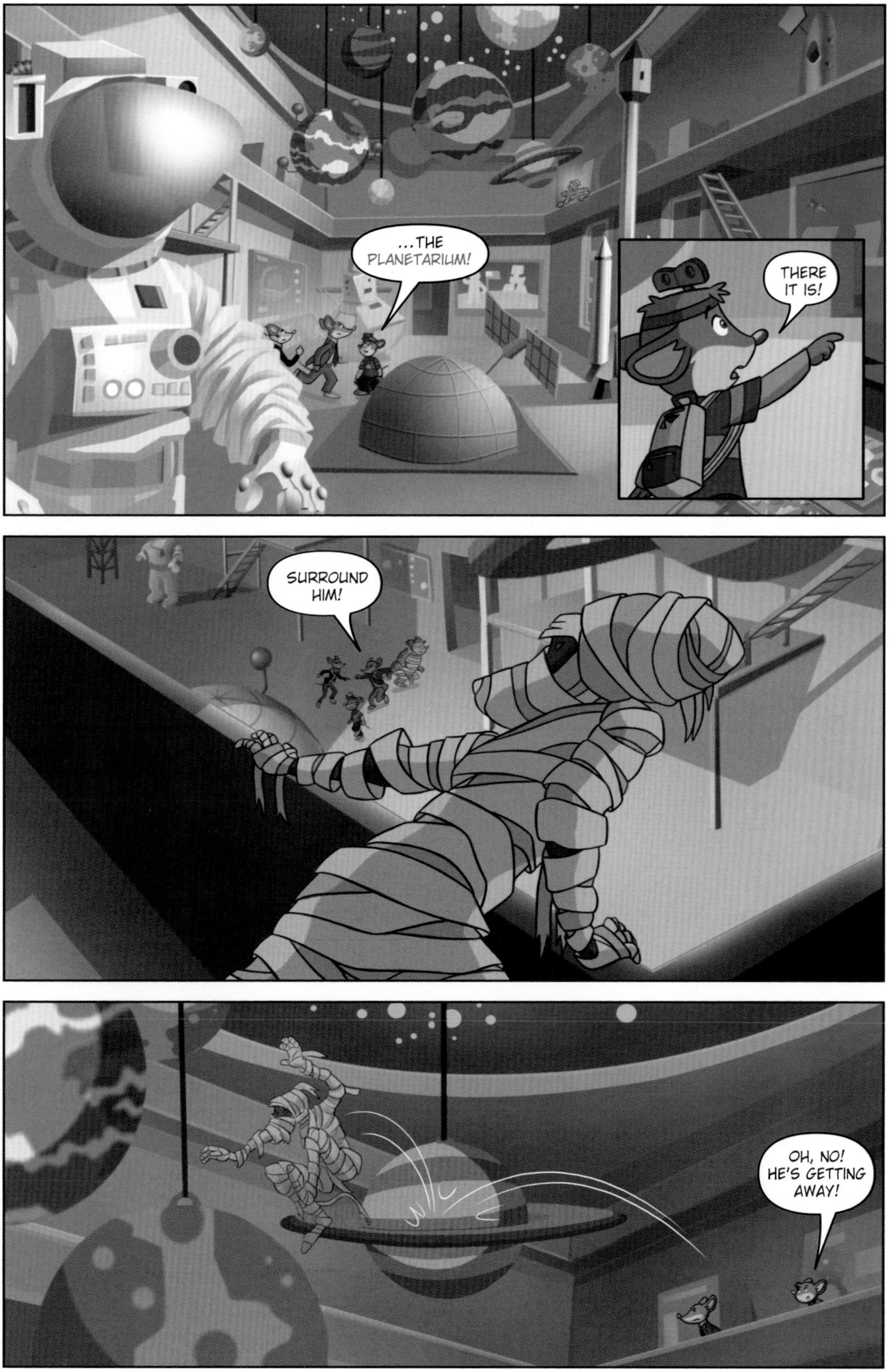
...THE PLANETARIUM!
THERE IT IS!
SURROUND HIM!
OH, NO! HE'S GETTING AWAY!

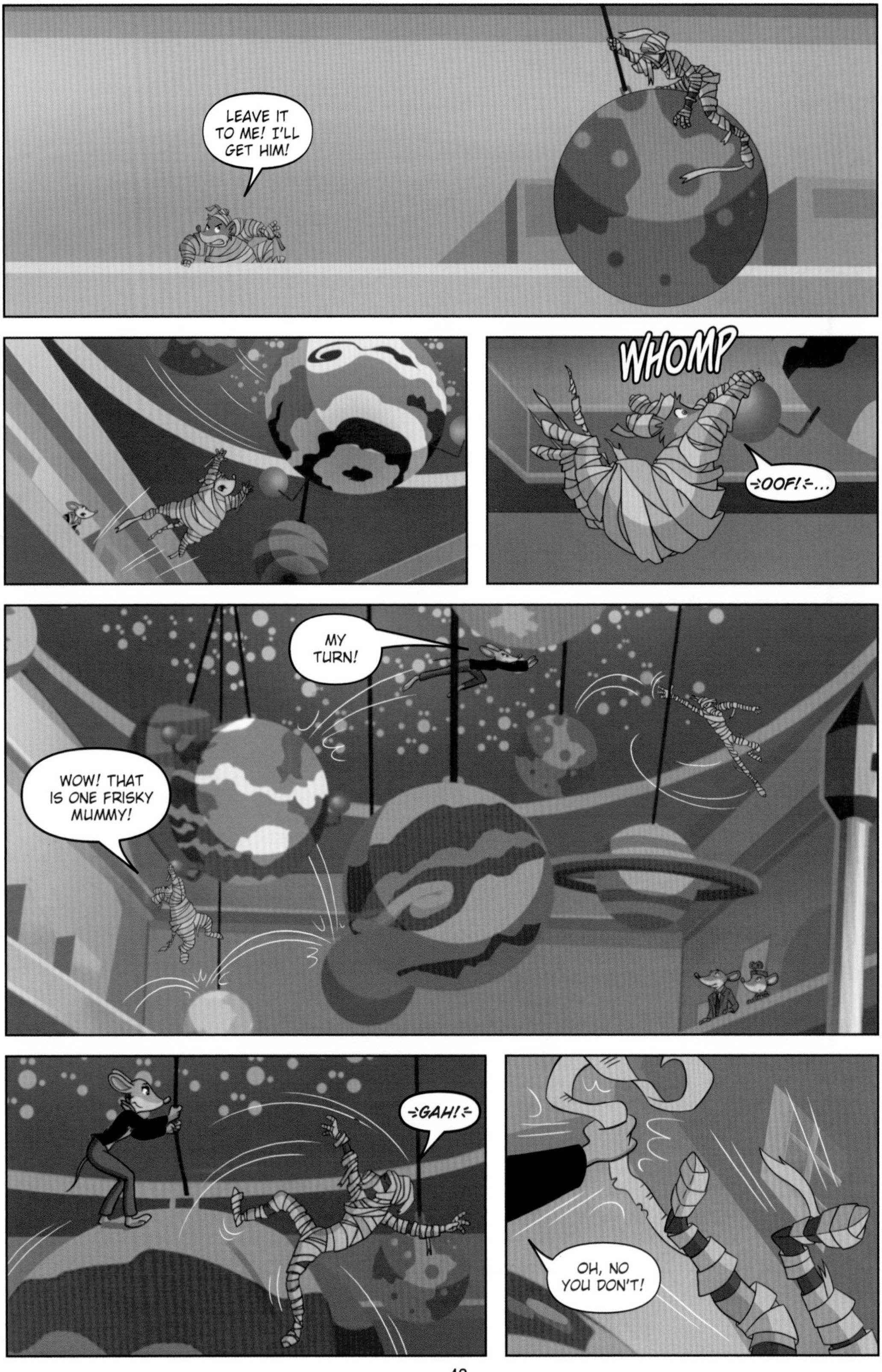
LEAVE IT TO ME! I'LL GET HIM!
WHOMP
OOF! ...
MY TURN!
WOW! THAT IS ONE FRISKY MUMMY!
GAH!
OH, NO YOU DON'T!

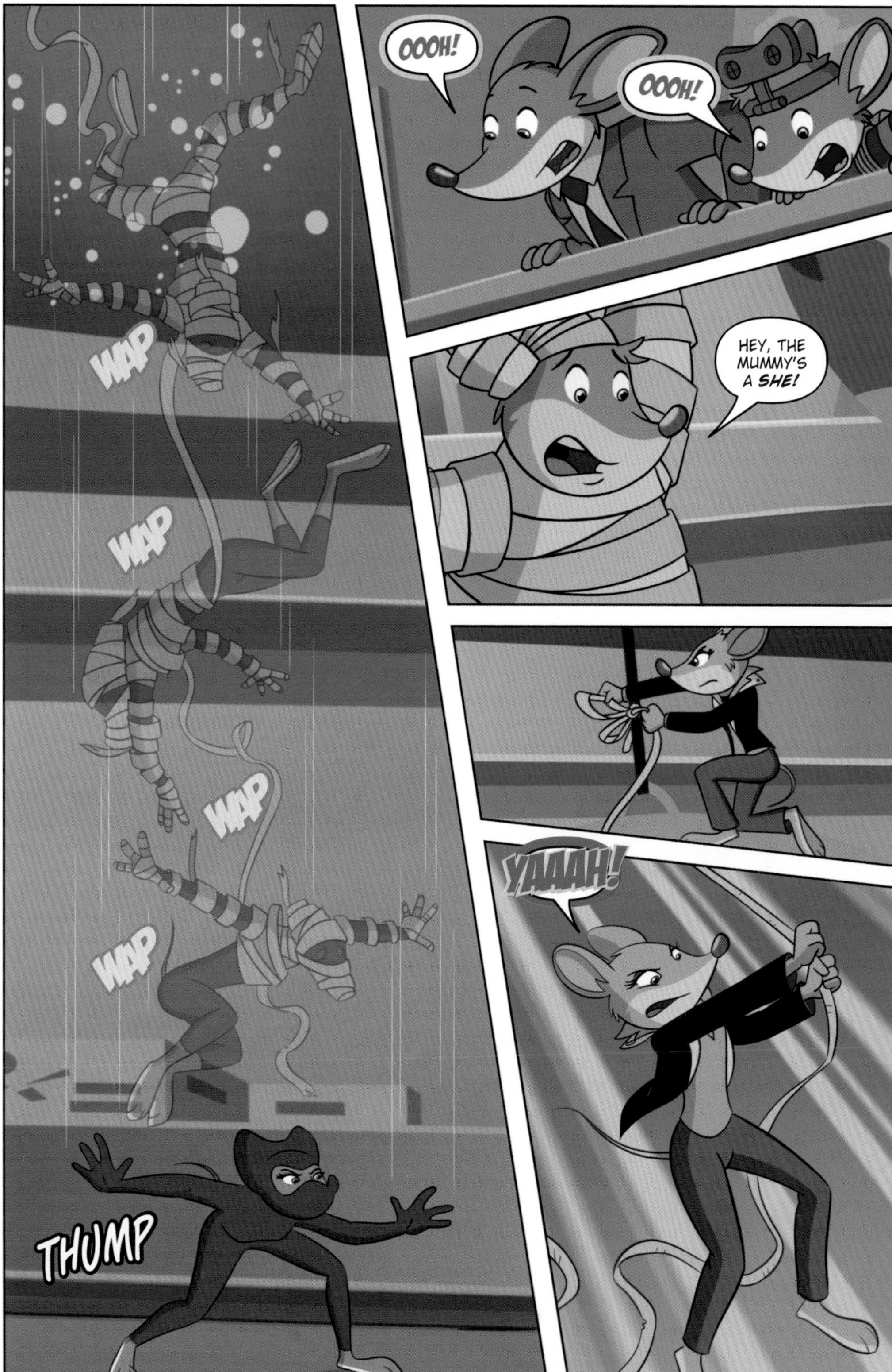
WAP
WAP
WAP
WAP
THUMP
OOOH!
OOOH!
HEY, THE MUMMY'S A SHE!
YAAAH!

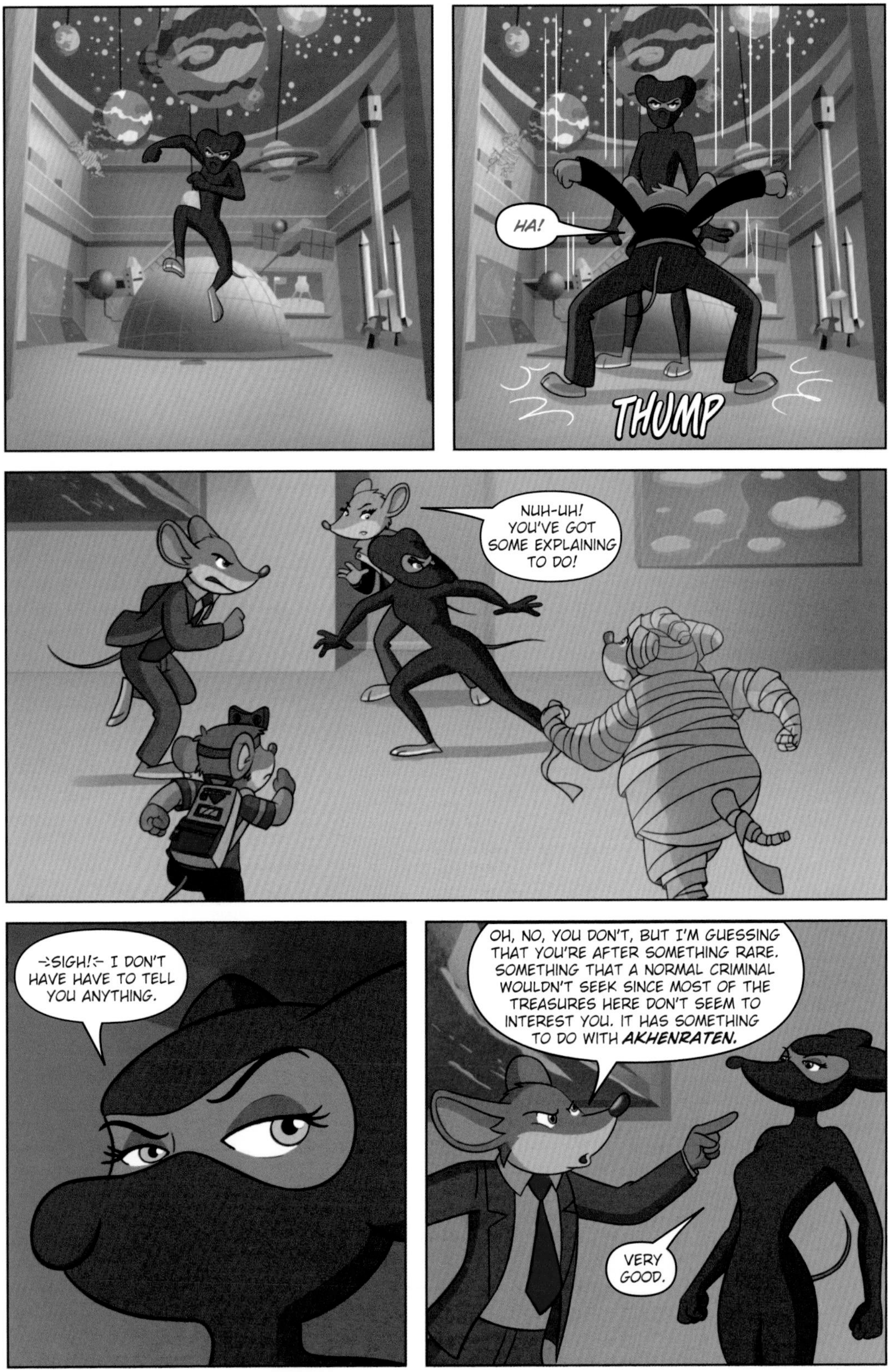
HA!
THUMP
NUH-UH! YOU'VE GOT SOME EXPLAINING TO DO!
–SIGH!– I DON'T HAVE HAVE TO TELL YOU ANYTHING.
OH, NO, YOU DON'T, BUT I'M GUESSING THAT YOU'RE AFTER SOMETHING RARE. SOMETHING THAT A NORMAL CRIMINAL WOULDN'T SEEK SINCE MOST OF THE TREASURES HERE DON'T SEEM TO INTEREST YOU. IT HAS SOMETHING TO DO WITH **AKHENRATEN.**
VERY GOOD.

YEAH, BUT WHO ARE YOU, *MUMMY-WOMAN?*

MY NAME IS **SHADOW.** AND I'VE BEEN SEEKING AKHENRATEN'S MOST VALUABLE TREASURE.

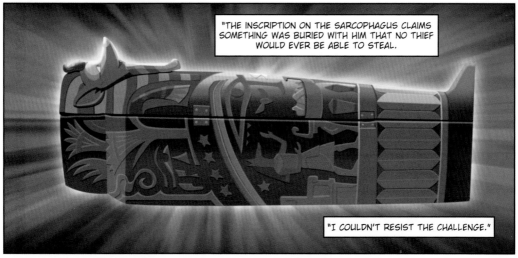

"THE INSCRIPTION ON THE SARCOPHAGUS CLAIMS SOMETHING WAS BURIED WITH HIM THAT NO THIEF WOULD EVER BE ABLE TO STEAL.

"I COULDN'T RESIST THE CHALLENGE."

HMMMM...

BLINK

AH-HA!

I KNOW WHAT IT IS **AND** WHY YOU COULDN'T FIND IT.

45

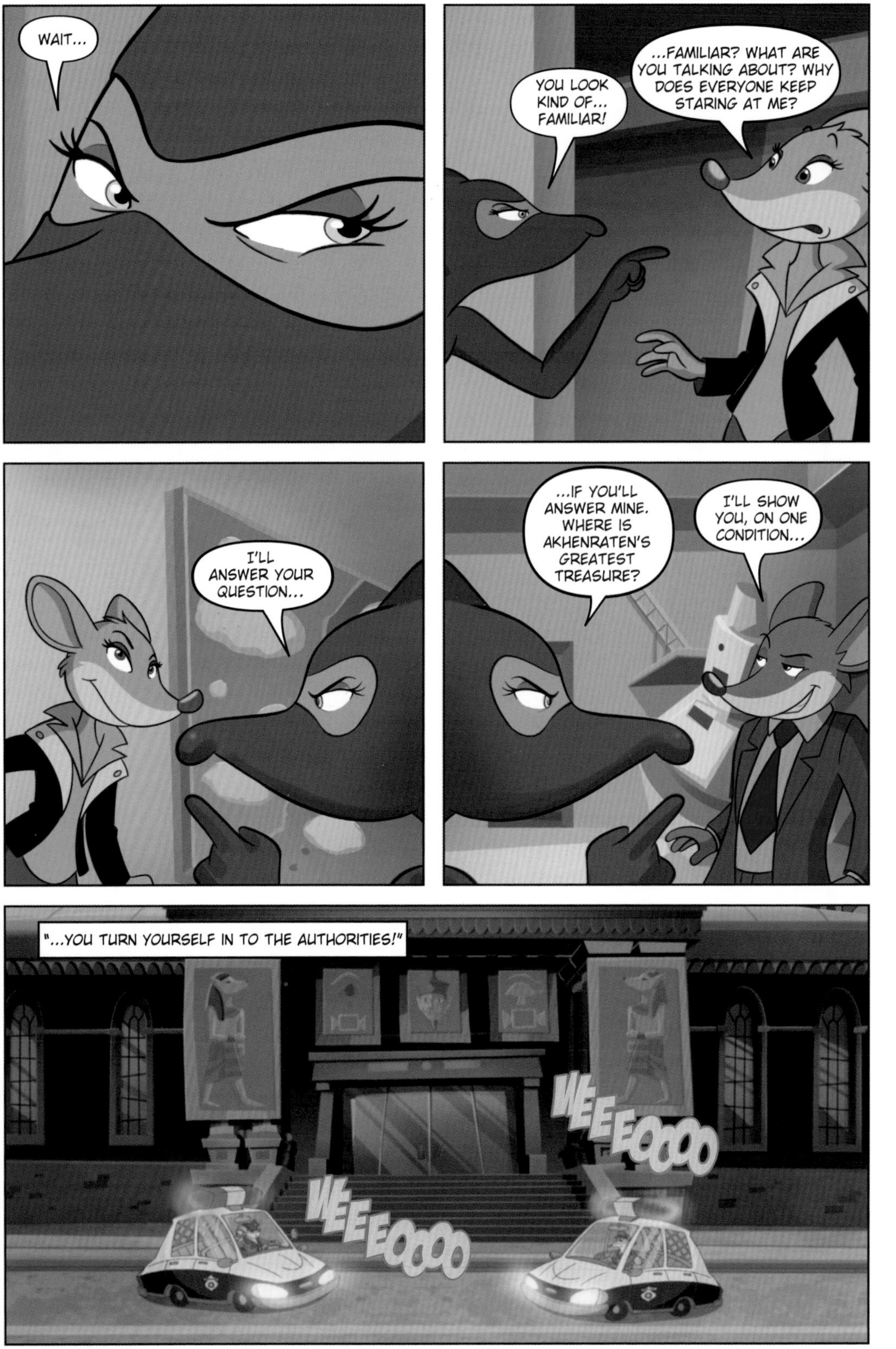
WAIT...
YOU LOOK KIND OF... FAMILIAR!
...FAMILIAR? WHAT ARE YOU TALKING ABOUT? WHY DOES EVERYONE KEEP STARING AT ME?
I'LL ANSWER YOUR QUESTION...
...IF YOU'LL ANSWER MINE. WHERE IS AKHENRATEN'S GREATEST TREASURE?
I'LL SHOW YOU, ON ONE CONDITION...
"...YOU TURN YOURSELF IN TO THE AUTHORITIES!"
WEEEOOOO
WEEEOOOO

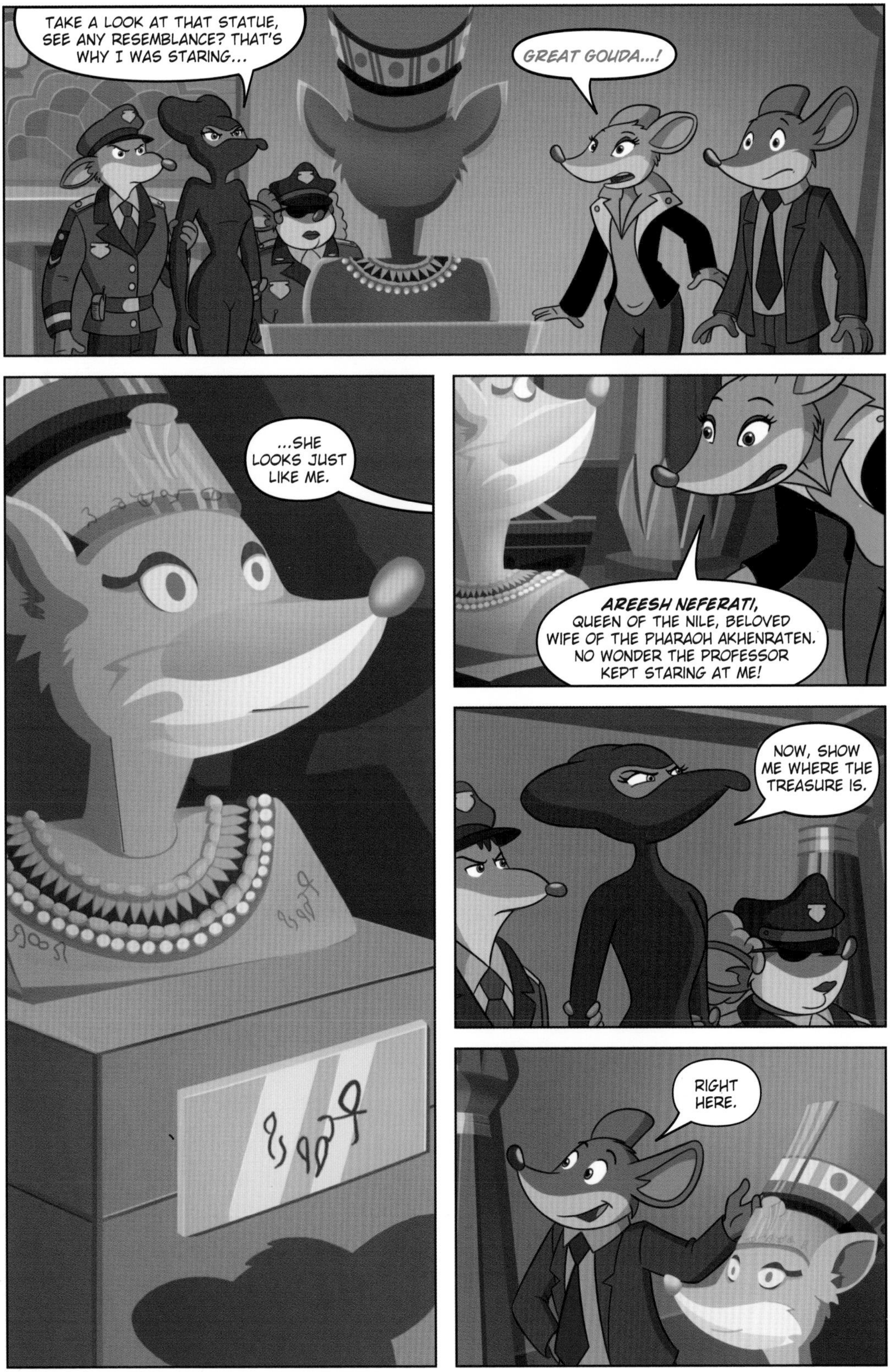
TAKE A LOOK AT THAT STATUE, SEE ANY RESEMBLANCE? THAT'S WHY I WAS STARING...
GREAT GOUDA...!
...SHE LOOKS JUST LIKE ME.
AREESH NEFERATI, QUEEN OF THE NILE, BELOVED WIFE OF THE PHARAOH AKHENRATEN. NO WONDER THE PROFESSOR KEPT STARING AT ME!
NOW, SHOW ME WHERE THE TREASURE IS.
RIGHT HERE.

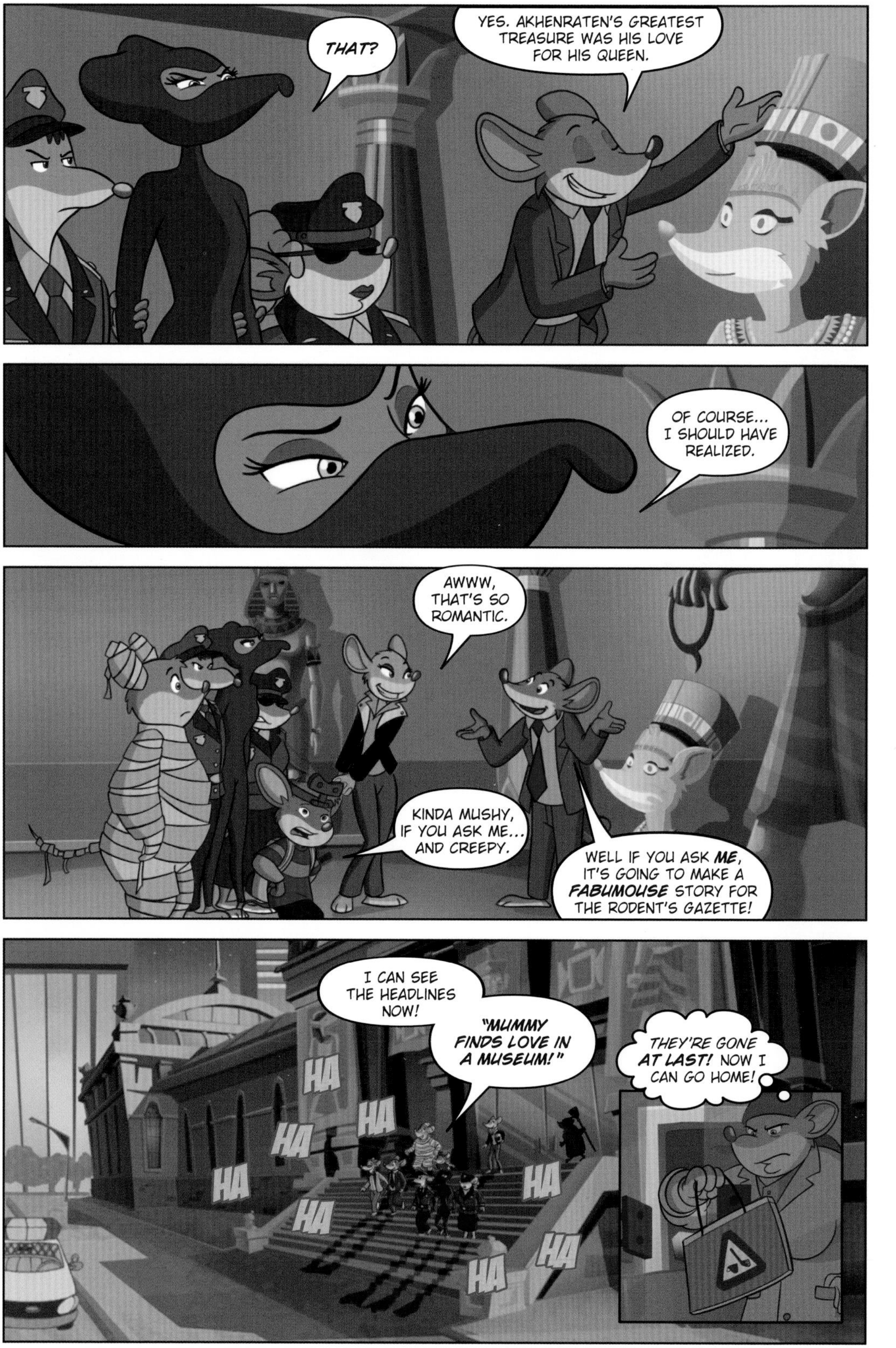
THAT?
YES. AKHENRATEN'S GREATEST TREASURE WAS HIS LOVE FOR HIS QUEEN.
OF COURSE... I SHOULD HAVE REALIZED.
AWWW, THAT'S SO ROMANTIC.
KINDA MUSHY, IF YOU ASK ME... AND CREEPY.
WELL IF YOU ASK **ME**, IT'S GOING TO MAKE A **FABUMOUSE** STORY FOR THE RODENT'S GAZETTE!
I CAN SEE THE HEADLINES NOW!
"MUMMY FINDS LOVE IN A MUSEUM!"
HA HA HA HA HA HA HA HA HA
THEY'RE GONE **AT LAST!** NOW I CAN GO HOME!

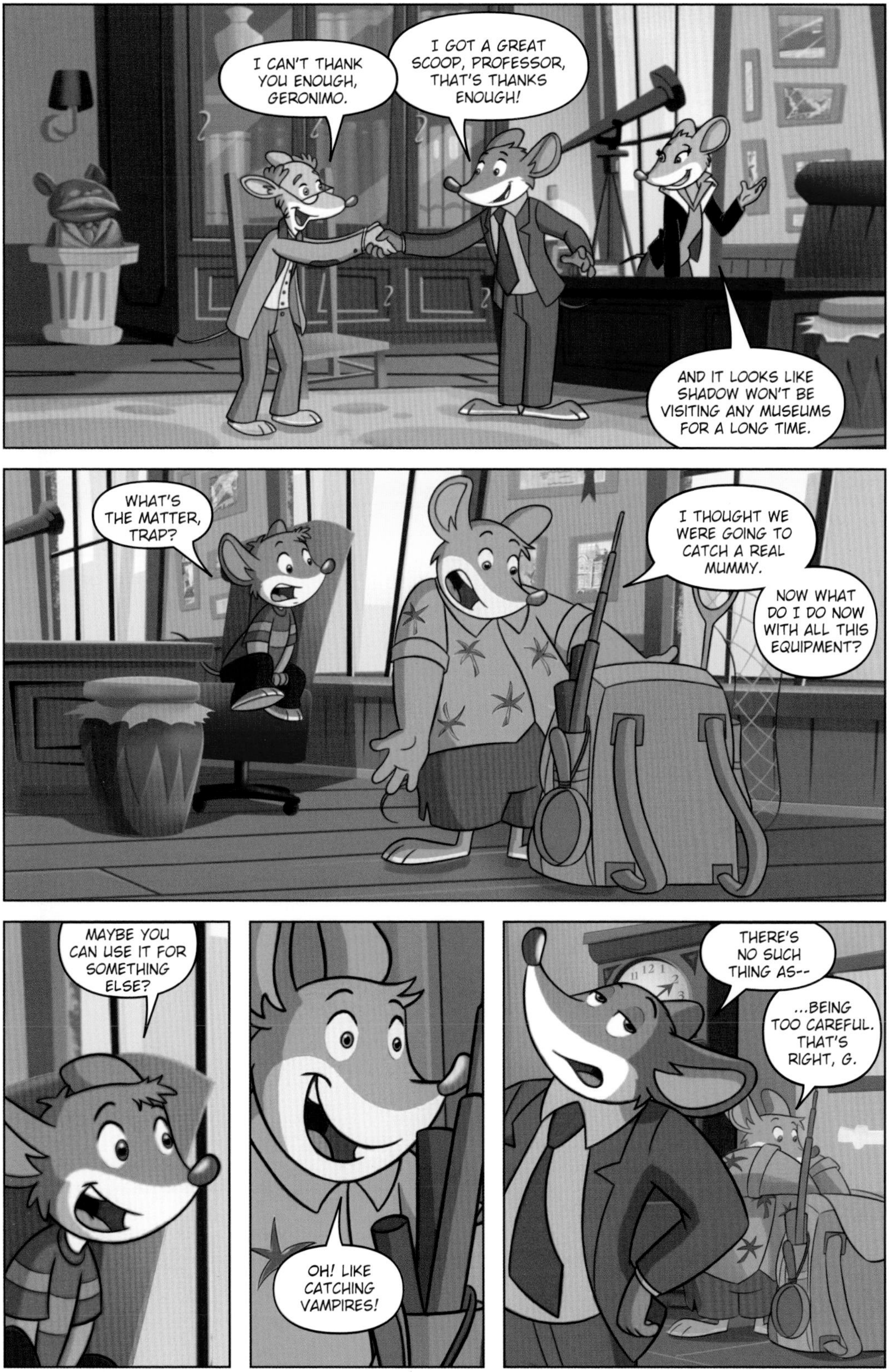
I CAN'T THANK YOU ENOUGH, GERONIMO.
I GOT A GREAT SCOOP, PROFESSOR, THAT'S THANKS ENOUGH!
AND IT LOOKS LIKE SHADOW WON'T BE VISITING ANY MUSEUMS FOR A LONG TIME.
WHAT'S THE MATTER, TRAP?
I THOUGHT WE WERE GOING TO CATCH A REAL MUMMY.
NOW WHAT DO I DO NOW WITH ALL THIS EQUIPMENT?
MAYBE YOU CAN USE IT FOR SOMETHING ELSE?
OH! LIKE CATCHING VAMPIRES!
THERE'S NO SUCH THING AS--
...BEING TOO CAREFUL. THAT'S RIGHT, G.

LUCKY FOR ME I HAVE ONE OF THESE.

A LIFE RAFT?!

YUP! VAMPIRES ARE TERRIFIED OF LIFE RAFTS.

SWWIIPP

NO, THEY'RE NOT!

OH!

FSSSSSSH

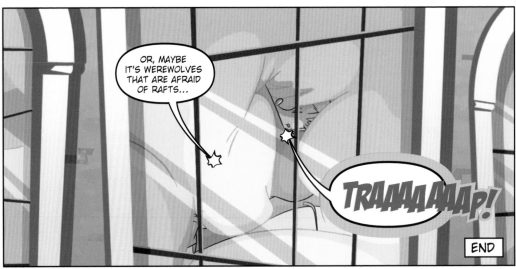

OR, MAYBE IT'S WEREWOLVES THAT ARE AFRAID OF RAFTS...

TRAAAAAAAP!

END

Watch Out For PAPERCUTZ™

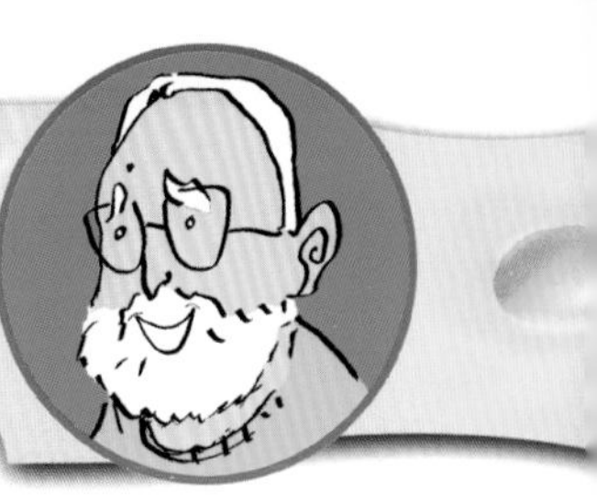

Welcome to the fun-and-fear-filled, family-focused, fourth GERONIMO STILTON REPORTER graphic novel, "The Mummy With No Name," the official comics adaptation of the fourth episode of *Geronimo Stilton* Season One, written by Kurt Weldon, brought to you by Papercutz—those tightly-wrapped friendly folks dedicated to publishing great graphic novels for all ages. I'm Salicrup, ***Jim Salicrup,*** the Editor-in-Chief and living-museum piece.

If you're already familiar with Geronimo Stilton, and all the ways you can enjoy his incredible adventures, feel free to skip ahead to the next paragraph. If you're new to the transmedia sensation that is Geronimo Stilton, allow me to offer up a crash course – a *Faster Class*, if you will – regarding this pop culture phenomenon. It all began with the long-running series – over 70 volumes, with more to come – of GERONIMO STILTON chapter books from our friends at Scholastic, and that's not counting such popular spin-off series such as GERONIMO STILTON AND THE FANTASY KINGDOM, GERONIMO STILTON JOURNEY THROUGH TIME, GERONIMO STILTON SPACEMICE, GERONIMO STILTON CAVEMICE, GERONIMO STILTON SPECIAL EDITION, THEA STILTON, and others. Papercutz (that's us) then joined in with a series of GERONIMO STILTON graphic novels, that featured Geronimo's adventures saving the future, by protecting the past, usually from those pesky Pirate Cats. That time-traveling series ran for nineteen volumes, which are now being collected in GERONIMO STILTON 3 IN 1, a new series that collects three GERONIMO STILTON graphic novels in each specially priced volume. Papercutz also publishes eight volumes of THEA STILTON, which featured the Thea Sisters – Colette, Nicky, Pamela, Paulina, and Violet – five fun, lively students at Mouseford Academy on Whale Island, who want to be real live journalists like their hero, Thea Stilton. Then there's this series, GERONIMO STILTON REPORTER, which brings you the official comics adaptations of the animated *Geronimo Stilton* TV series, seen on Netflix and Amazon Prime. So, if you like Geronimo Stilton in this series, there are plenty more tales of Geronimo and his friends and family out there – at your favorite booksellers, libraries, and on TV.

A character such as Geronimo Stilton is very special, and there are certain core values that are always present in each and every Geronimo Stilton story. You can find those values described in great detail on geronimostilton.com in a section called *The Philosophy of Geronimo Stilton.* We've also been talking about those values, in the Watch Out for Papercutz pages in GERONIMO STILTON 3 IN 1, and here in GERONIMO STILTON REPORTER. This time, we'd like to talk about…

GERONIMO STILTON AND HIS ADVERSARIES
Geronimo's attitude when facing his adversaries is never one of violent confrontation but always of competition with fair play, in the sense of civility and respect for others. He often considers the teasing from his enemies as an opportunity to practice his patience.

What a coincidence that this is the portion of *The Philosophy of Geronimo Stilton* that I would be commenting on now. Let me explain. Just a few weeks ago, I was representing Papercutz, along with several of our writers and artists, at the Papercutz booth at the ALA (the American Library Association) Annual Conference and Exhibition held in Washington D.C. Somehow or other, I got drawn into a debate with the creators of the Papercutz graphic novel series, THE ONLY LIVING GIRL, David Gallaher, writer, and Steve Ellis, artist. David was making the case that Marvel's Spider-Man, despite years of Peter Parker (Spidey's secret identity) being teased as a teenager himself – he was called "Puny Parker" – was, in fact, a bully himself. As someone who had written and edited many Spider-Man stories, I must admit, I was somewhat shocked by Mr. Gallaher's claim. And while Steve and I attempted to defend Spider-Man/ Peter Parker, David would continue to point out there was simply no excuse for a hero to ever resort to insulting anyone. For example, was it ever necessary for Spidey to call his massive foe, the Kingpin, "Fatso"? I always took it as part of Spidey's sense of humor – something along the lines of the "insult" comedy of comedians such as Don Rickles or Johnny Carson – or simply trash-talking, in the spirit of professional wrestling. But after giving David's argument ample thought, I asked myself how would Spidey's co-creator, Stan Lee – the guy who wrote some of the very lines to which David was objecting – respond to such criticism. While Stan's no longer with us, I did know and work with Mr. Lee for many years, and I honestly think I know what his response would've been. Stan would never wish to hurt a single person's feelings, and if certain words (such as "Fatso") would hurt a single Spidey-fan, then he would no longer use those words. By the way, having just seen *Spider-Man: Far From Home*, I think it's safe to say that the Marvel Cinematic Universe incarnation of Spider-Man wouldn't ever be intentionally hurtful either.

Which brings us back to Geronimo Stilton. His "sense of civility and respect for others" is yet another admirable aspect of this incredible character. It may seem silly to be inspired by a mouse, but when he embraces such noble and thoughtful ideas, how can we not try to follow his example? It's not easy at times, but if Geronimo can do it, I will attempt to try harder in my own life to be more understanding, and most importantly, respectful.

Gee, I got so carried away regarding *The Philosophy of Geronimo Stilton,* that I forgot to mention that if you're looking for a mummy **with** a name, you need look no further than the HOTEL TRANSYLVANIA graphic novel series from Papercutz. There you'll happily find Murray the mummy, and he's the life of the party – a mad monster party, that is! He, along with Drac, Mavis, Johnny, Dennis, Frank, Wayne, and Griffin, the stars from the hit animated HOTEL TRANSYLVANIA movies, star in all-new adventures. Although we can't promise that Drac will be embracing "a sense of civility and respect for others." For that, you may want to keep an eye out for GERONIMO STILTON REPORTER #5 "Barry the Moustache," which is coming soon to booksellers and libraries everywhere. Check out the special preview on the following pages. And don't miss Geronimo's animated adventures on Netflix and Amazon Prime! See you in the future!

Respectfully yours,

Jim

STAY IN TOUCH!

EMAIL:	salicrup@papercutz.com
WEB:	papercutz.com
TWITTER:	@papercutzgn
INSTAGRAM:	@papercutzgn
FACEBOOK:	PAPERCUTZGRAPHICNOVELS
SNAIL MAIL:	Papercutz, 160 Broadway, Suite 700, East Wing, New York, NY 10038

Special Preview of GERONIMO STILTON REPORTER Graphic Novel #5 "Barry the Moustache"!

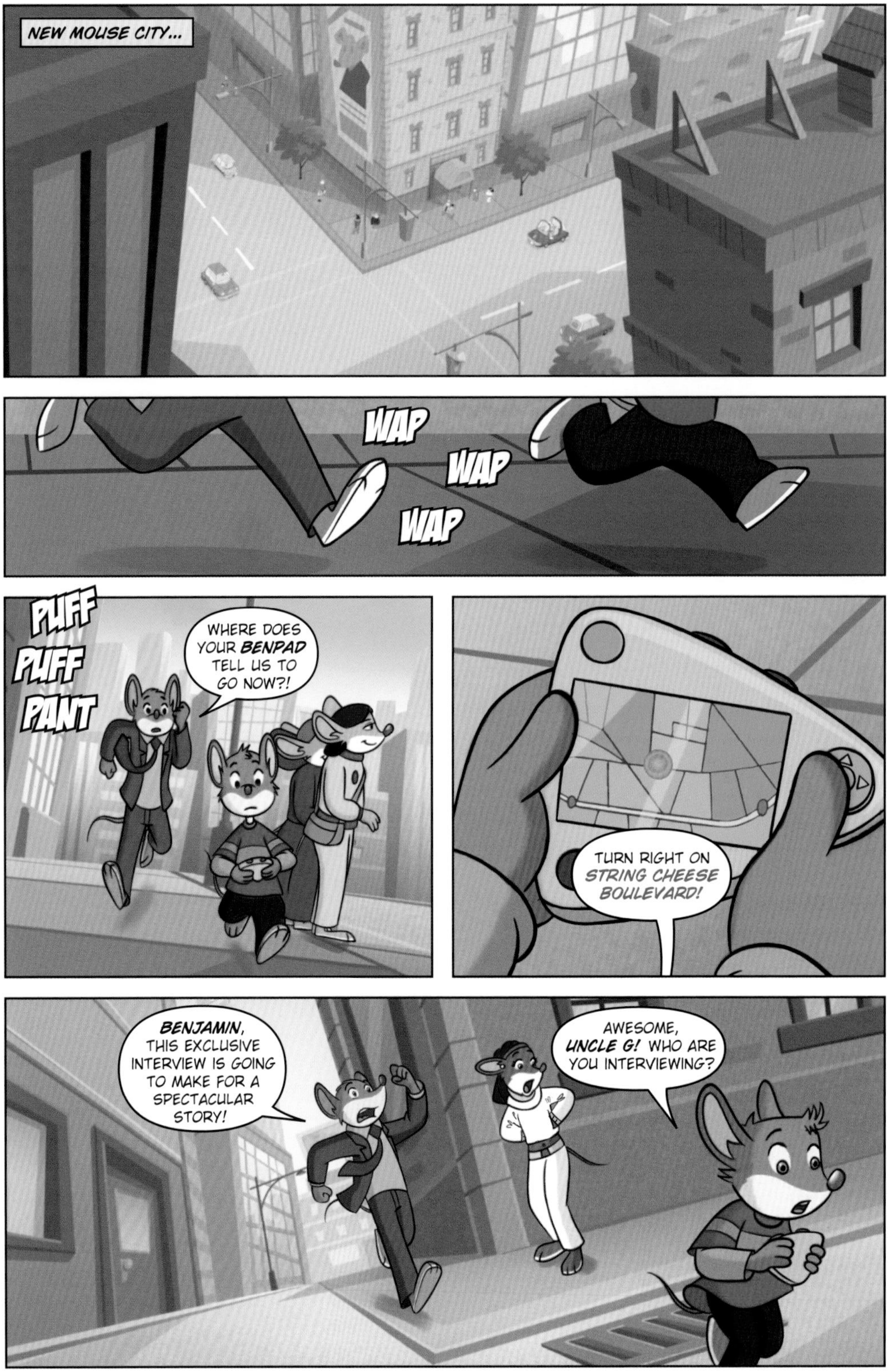

NEW MOUSE CITY...
WAP
WAP
WAP
PUFF
PUFF
PANT
WHERE DOES YOUR BENPAD TELL US TO GO NOW?!
TURN RIGHT ON STRING CHEESE BOULEVARD!
BENJAMIN, THIS EXCLUSIVE INTERVIEW IS GOING TO MAKE FOR A SPECTACULAR STORY!
AWESOME, UNCLE G! WHO ARE YOU INTERVIEWING?

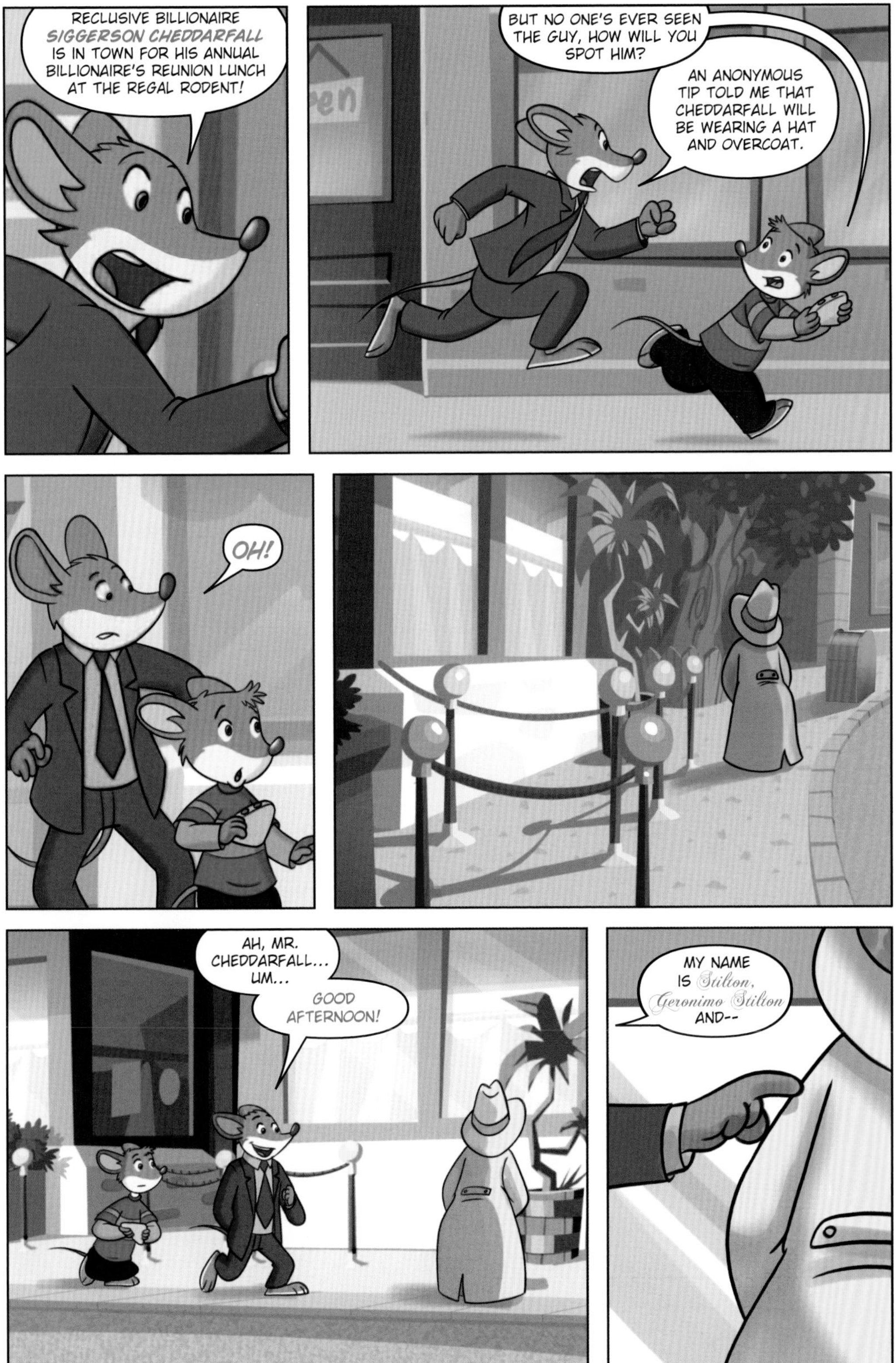

RECLUSIVE BILLIONAIRE SIGGERSON CHEDDARFALL IS IN TOWN FOR HIS ANNUAL BILLIONAIRE'S REUNION LUNCH AT THE REGAL RODENT!
BUT NO ONE'S EVER SEEN THE GUY, HOW WILL YOU SPOT HIM?
AN ANONYMOUS TIP TOLD ME THAT CHEDDARFALL WILL BE WEARING A HAT AND OVERCOAT.
OH!
AH, MR. CHEDDARFALL... UM...
GOOD AFTERNOON!
MY NAME IS Stilton, Geronimo Stilton AND--

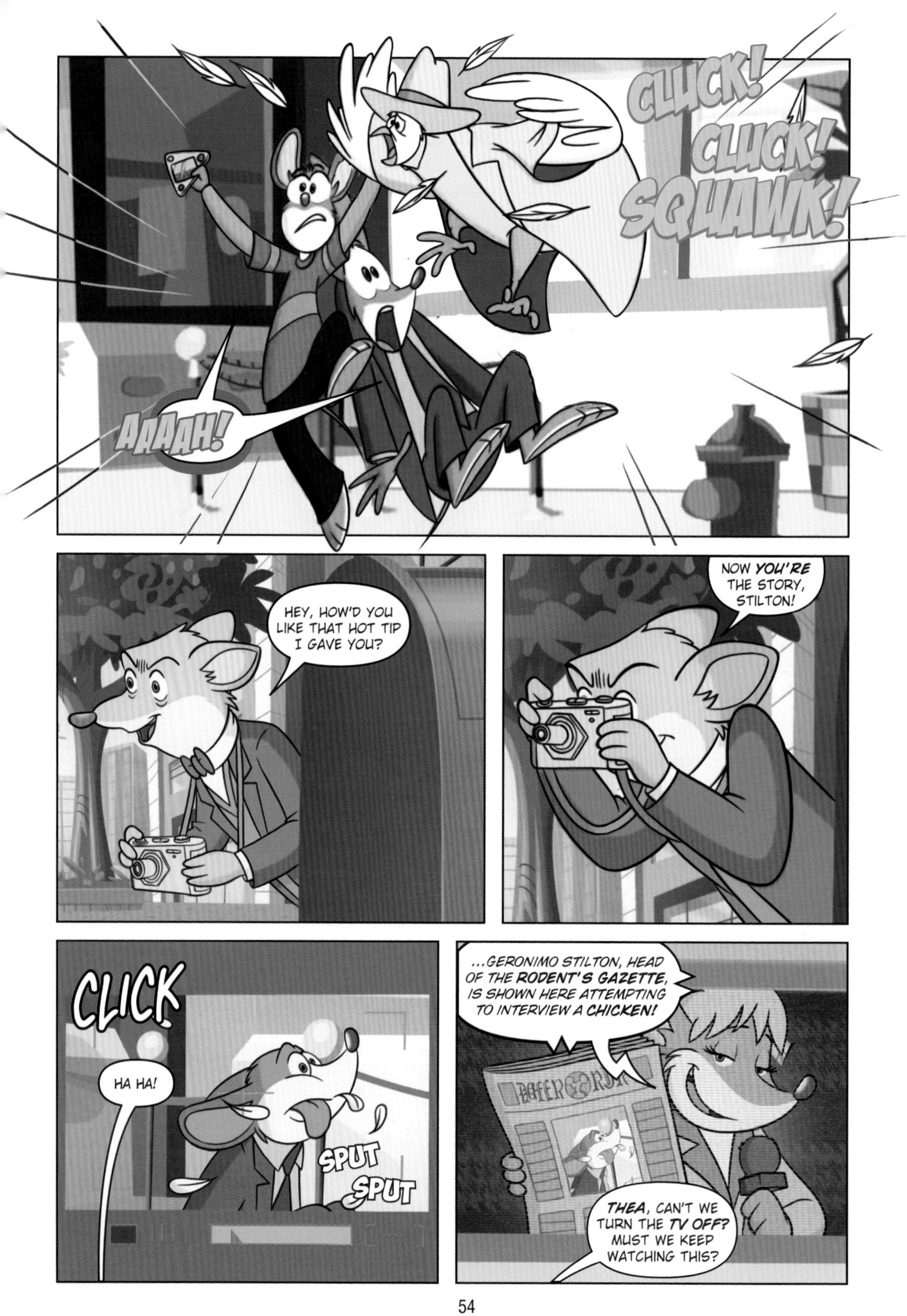
CLUCK! CLUCK! SQUAWK!
AAAAH!
HEY, HOW'D YOU LIKE THAT HOT TIP I GAVE YOU?
NOW YOU'RE THE STORY, STILTON!
CLICK
HA HA!
SPUT SPUT
...GERONIMO STILTON, HEAD OF THE RODENT'S GAZETTE, IS SHOWN HERE ATTEMPTING TO INTERVIEW A CHICKEN!
THEA, CAN'T WE TURN THE TV OFF? MUST WE KEEP WATCHING THIS?

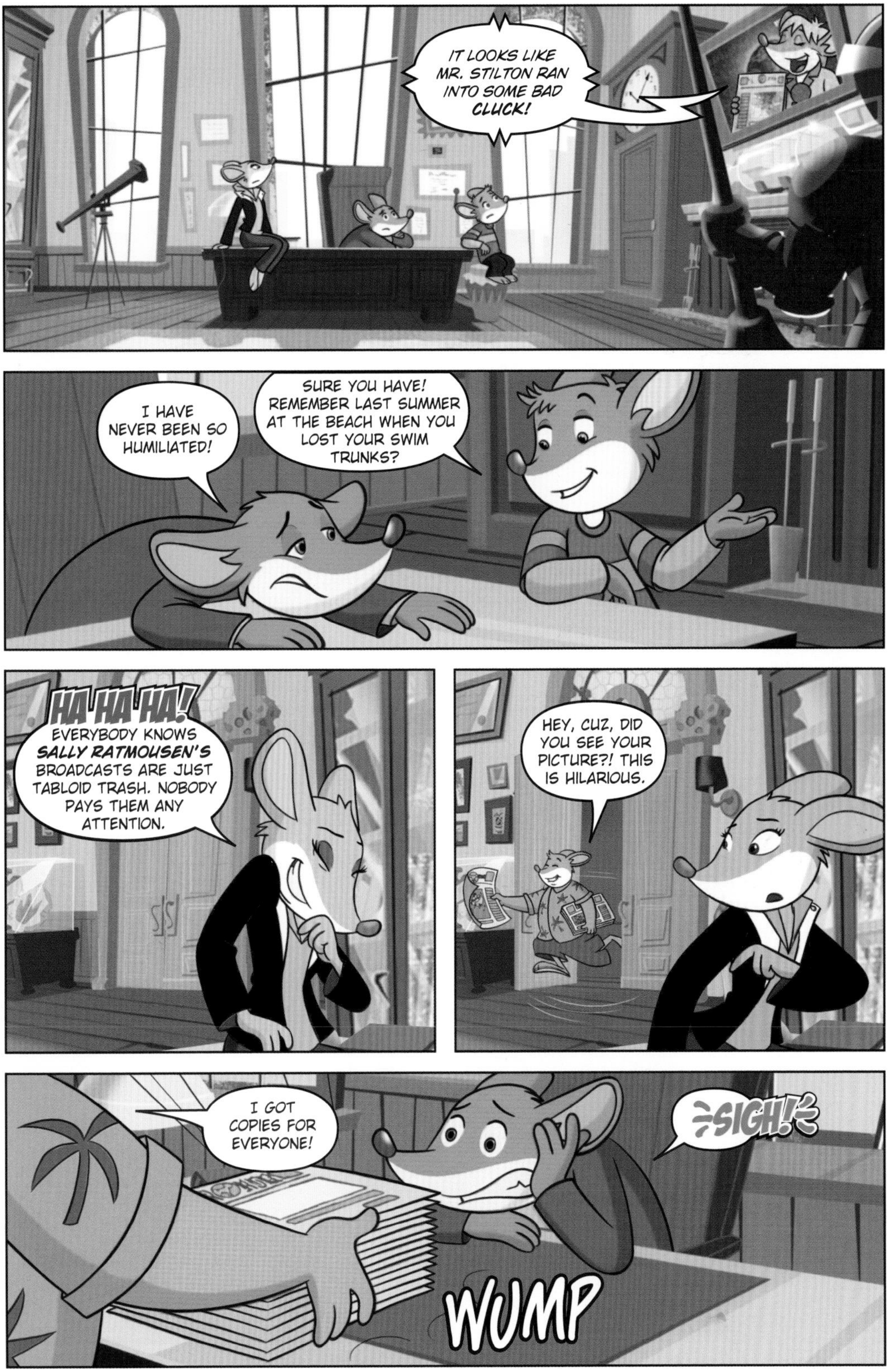
IT LOOKS LIKE MR. STILTON RAN INTO SOME BAD CLUCK!
I HAVE NEVER BEEN SO HUMILIATED!
SURE YOU HAVE! REMEMBER LAST SUMMER AT THE BEACH WHEN YOU LOST YOUR SWIM TRUNKS?
HA HA HA!
EVERYBODY KNOWS SALLY RATMOUSEN'S BROADCASTS ARE JUST TABLOID TRASH. NOBODY PAYS THEM ANY ATTENTION.
HEY, CUZ, DID YOU SEE YOUR PICTURE?! THIS IS HILARIOUS.
I GOT COPIES FOR EVERYONE!
SIGH!
WUMP

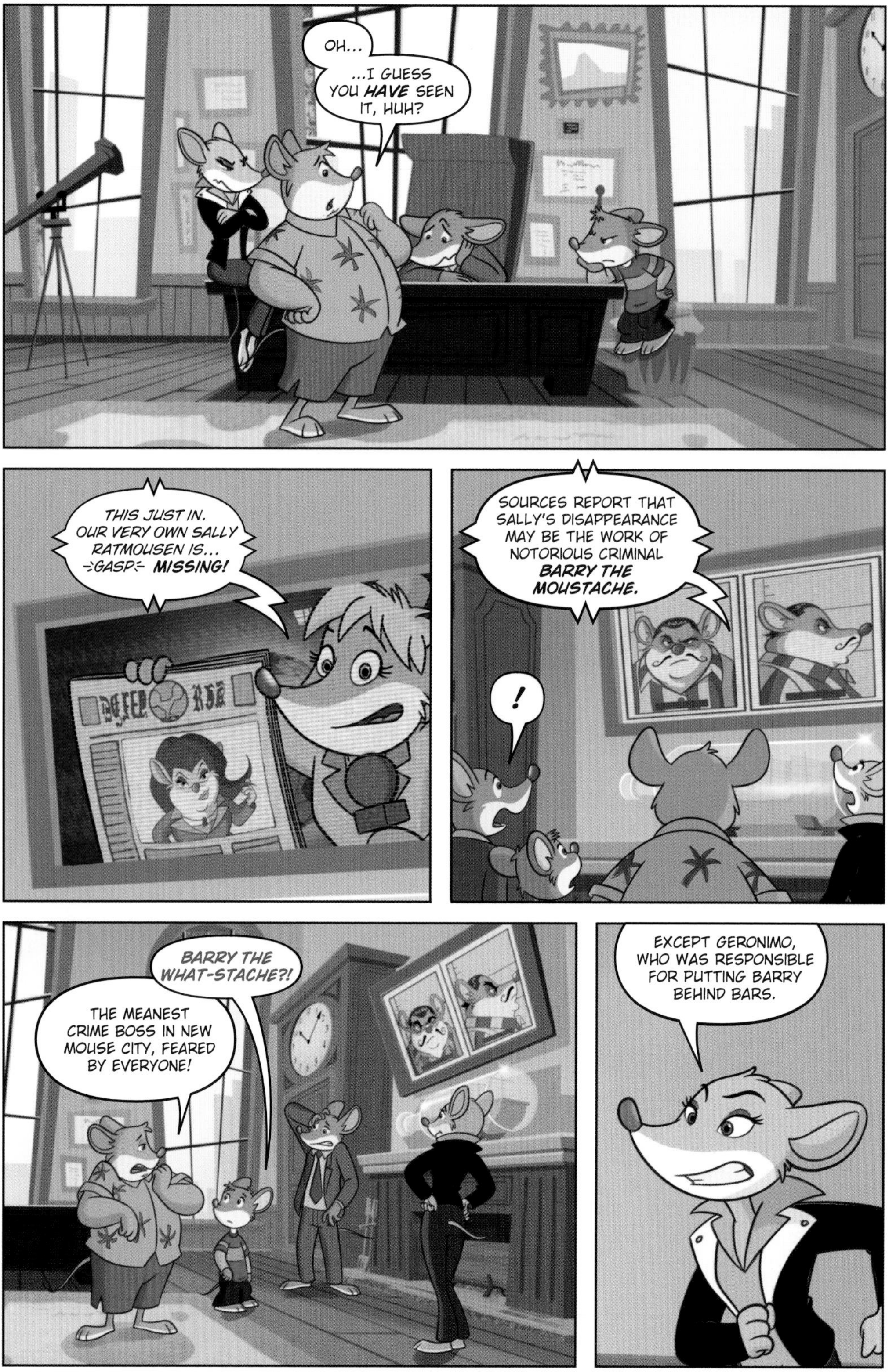
OH...
...I GUESS YOU HAVE SEEN IT, HUH?
THIS JUST IN. OUR VERY OWN SALLY RATMOUSEN IS... -GASP- MISSING!
SOURCES REPORT THAT SALLY'S DISAPPEARANCE MAY BE THE WORK OF NOTORIOUS CRIMINAL BARRY THE MOUSTACHE.
!
BARRY THE WHAT-STACHE?!
THE MEANEST CRIME BOSS IN NEW MOUSE CITY, FEARED BY EVERYONE!
EXCEPT GERONIMO, WHO WAS RESPONSIBLE FOR PUTTING BARRY BEHIND BARS.

Don't Miss GERONIMO STILTON REPORTER #5 "Barry the Moustache"! Coming soon!

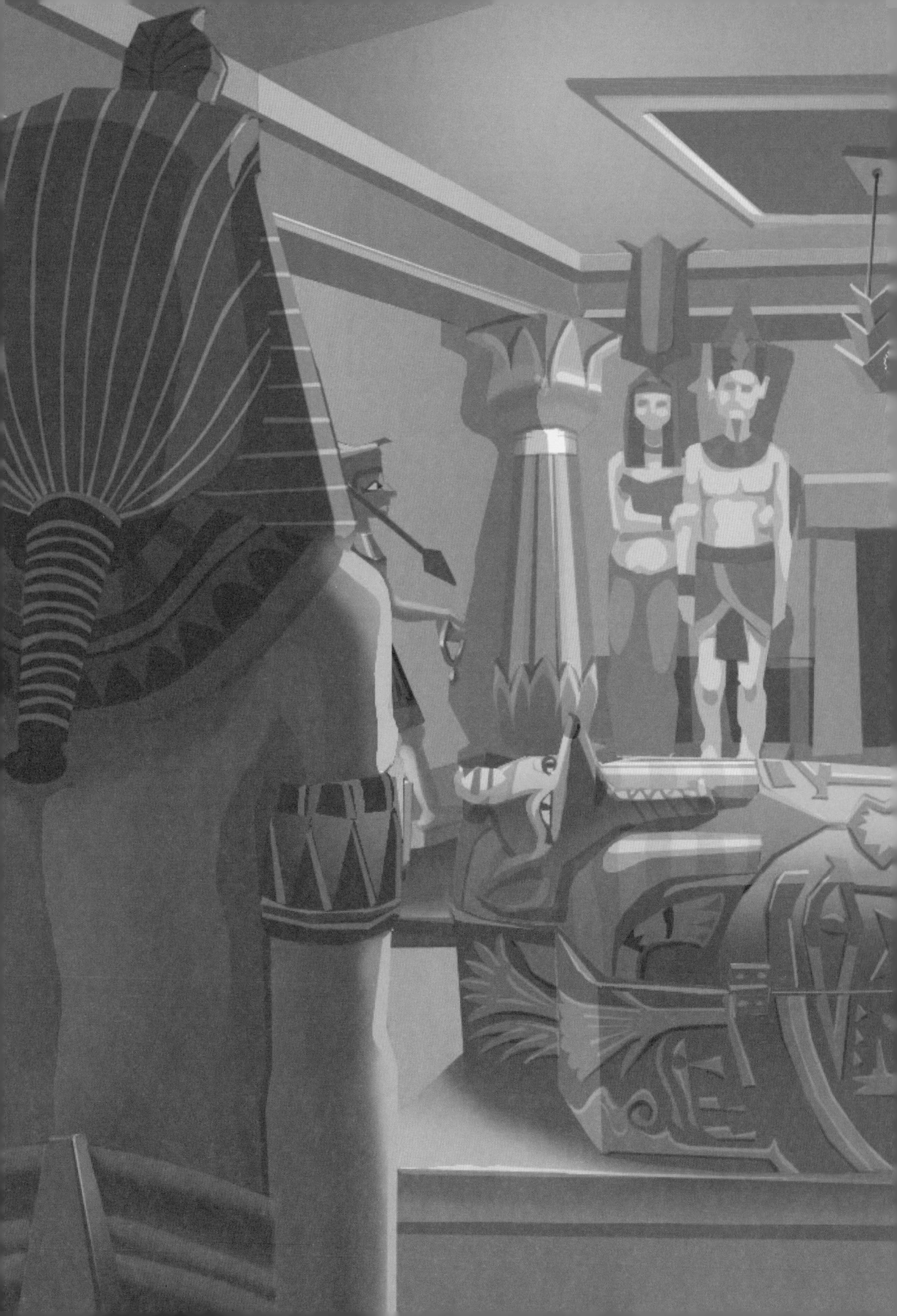